To Wendy,

Here's to a soul enriching
African adventure in April
with elders.

Alyson

When the River Wakes Up

Alyson Quinn

Hamilton Books

A member of
Rowman & Littlefield
Lanham • Boulder • New York • Toronto • Plymouth, UK

Copyright © 2014 by Hamilton Books
4501 Forbes Boulevard, Suite 200, Lanham, Maryland 20706
Hamilton Books Aquisitions Department (301) 459-3366

10 Thornbury Road, Plymouth PL6 7PP, United Kingdom

All rights reserved
Printed in the United States of America
British Library Cataloguing in Publication Information Available

Library of Congress Control Number: 2014942362
ISBN: 978-0-7618-6426-4 (paper : alk. paper)—ISBN: 978-0-7618-6427-1 (electronic)

∞™ The paper used in this publication meets the minimum requirements of American
National Standard for Information Sciences Permanence of Paper for Printed Library
Materials, ANSI/NISO Z39.48-1992.

To Stanley, Robin and Zukah

I am eternally grateful for your love and guidance.

Contents

Acknowledgments

Firstly I would like to acknowledge the staff of Hamilton Books, I am so grateful for your support regarding my novel *When the River Wakes Up*. I would especially like to thank assistant acquisitions editor Nicolette Amstutz who brings tremendous skill and enthusiasm to her job—thank you Nicolette. I would also like to acknowledge a tireless Trish O'Connor for her bird's eye view, her precision, intuition and dedication in editing the novel; I am deeply appreciative of your work Trish and commitment to excellence.

Thanks too for friends Steve, Terry and Nicola for assisting me in choosing the final photo. As always thank you to family and friends who support me beautifully on my creative path.

Chapter 1

Abigail nestled next to her mother like an animal burrowing for warmth and shelter. She felt their hips joined and their shoulders glued together. Instinctively, she filled every gap between them, drawing from her mother's body the strength she needed, strength she could not find within herself right now.

She looked over her shoulder and briefly scanned her family for any sign of distress. She noted her father's bowed head, his moist eyes, his wet eyelashes. She wanted to comfort him, but she didn't know how. She felt the tears sitting in the back of her eyes, somehow frozen; she didn't know what to do with her hands. She played with her black skirt lining, pulling it down, tugging at it. Her hands couldn't stop moving as she looked at her beloved aunt Robin lying there in a wooden casket. The family and her uncle Peter had all peered in the casket together as soon as they arrived. Her father had touched Aunt Robin's inert hand, then picked it up and pushed back her limp brown hair, brushing her cheeks with the back of his hand. Her curls were flattened; death had taken the life out of her hair, too. Abigail felt her own body go stiff when the hand just fell back like a dead snake. She wanted to collapse over Aunt Robin's body and ask her where she had gone. She wanted Aunt Robin to wake up, sit up and tell her she was OK after all. Abigail watched for a slither of movement, but Aunt Robin did nothing, just lay there. Had she gone to heaven? If she was there, what was she doing right now? These questions were overwhelming Abigail, and she felt desperate for answers. She instinctively reached for her mother's hand as soon as she saw Aunt Robin's mouth, open and inert. Her eyes were closed but the expression on her face was haunting, as if it spoke a powerful language all of its own. Aunt Robin looked taken off guard, surprised, unprepared for the moment, frozen for all time. Uncle Peter then bent over too and touched her shoulder, his face similar to hers, frozen and shocked, but with a bit more life, Abigail

1

noted. His brown eyes seemed to have sunk somewhere far away, lost, the dark shadows under them emphasizing their hollowness. Abigail had never seen him look so bad, and wondered how he would cope when he went home to Canada.

Abigail looked up and took in all of the church surroundings. Even though she came regularly on Sundays, somehow it felt different today. Everything had more meaning now: Jesus dead on the cross, was he with Aunt Robin in heaven? The organ music filled the space; the notes chipped away at the wall protecting Abigail's heart. She forgot the name of the song but she knew it well. Aunt Robin would put it on in the morning just before the family sat down for breakfast. Her love of music followed her like a twin; her head would fall back with delight when the violin crescendo peaked, and her face looked transported to a new place, a different destination. Was that heaven?

Abigail had always looked forward to Aunt Robin's visit when she came all the way from Canada to Zimbabwe-Rhodesia. Every year as soon as New Year celebrations were over, Abigail knew it wouldn't be long before the family would be heading out to the airport to pick up Aunt Robin. She liked it when Aunt Robin came alone, and left her husband Peter behind to look after their house and garden. She had left her husband behind last year; Abigail was thrilled when she did the same this year. For Abigail, that meant more time for just them. They had already spent time going for walks in the bush, checking out the frogs at the river, and she was able to hear some of Aunt Robin's stories from Canada. Abigail loved the one about the bear that came into their log cabin in the wilderness and rummaged through the kitchen before it left. Aunt Robin talked about how frightened she and Uncle Peter had been; they bolted their bedroom door while the bear crashed about. Another favorite was when they saw a pod of whales right next to their boat, and they followed them for ages. She liked nature tales from somewhere else. Aunt Robin's stories were so numerous that Abigail started to piece together a life in a land that seemed so distant, it seemed almost not of earth, but in another galaxy. Fir trees everywhere, on every mountain. How could you see horizons if it was always fir trees? She imagined everyone living in darkness in the forest, a bit like a cave dweller, seeing the light only when they escaped. She couldn't even imagine leaving the place where she lived. Even though it felt isolated, apart from the world, still it was her home; the birds, animals and all the people, this was her place.

"We are gathered here together to mourn the loss ..." the priest had started the sermon. Abigail stared at his face, wondering if he had any idea what this meant to her. His mouth formed the words, but his face was almost devoid of expression. This is what she didn't like about church: everyone seemed to be saying all these important things; but they said them as if they were trying to join Jesus on the cross. Their expressions appeared as dead as

Jesus' lifeless form. Her world was confusing enough; so she found herself befriending people who felt things strongly, and said them with expressions on their faces, like people living what they were saying. That's what she loved about her parents and Aunt Robin: everyone said exactly what they meant, and she could see they meant it because their faces matched what they said. She had started to distrust people who looked as if they were playing a part, just like this priest; his face wasn't sad, why? Her aunt was frozen right now in that wooden box and there was nothing, absolutely nothing that was going to bring Aunt Robin back so she could go for a walk with Abigail this afternoon. The priest's mutterings floated above Abigail's head like an ethereal mist evaporating into nothingness.

She remembered her father's face when he had walked out of the room at the hospital and told her, her brother and sister that Aunt Robin had had a heart attack. There was so much pain in his blue eyes that she immediately closed her eyes for what seemed like ages. His whole body had bent over like a tree scraping the earth with its branches. He said softly that Aunt Robin had had a weak heart for some time, and that she was now in peace. In peace? What about Abigail? Her own heart felt as if it were under attack, trapped behind a wall. Was it broken? How would she know? She didn't want to ask her parents now, not when they too were also dealing with Aunt Robin lying there, her pale skin a strange blue color, her mouth wide open so a fly could buzz around inside with no one to chase it out.

"We will now sing hymn number 52 in the red book," the priest declared. His brown eyes looked up over his half-lens glasses briefly, and he threw his right arm up so his pale flabby pink skin was revealed from under his vast white robe. Then he raised the book high into the air in a gesture of control over the masses. Abigail saw her mother reach for the book with her black-gloved hand and scan the pages. She gestured to Abigail to stand, and placed the book in view of both of them and put her arm securely around her. Abigail felt her body lean back into her mother's; she felt the strength in her mother's body, her fingers gently brushing her shoulder as if to rub her distress away. As she sang, the music seemed to worm into her heart, tears started to form in her eyes, a tear dropped onto the hymn page and she felt her mother squeeze her shoulder harder, as if to help her to squeeze more tears out. Fear rose inside, and the waterfall behind her eyes felt so big she didn't know whether she would ever be able to stop.

Aunt Robin was one of her best friends. She always seemed to know her, understand her, and she always seemed to say the right thing. Abigail had never imagined facing the New Year without Aunt Robin. How would she cope without her? Why did these things have to happen? Why was her world such a strange world? Why didn't she understand what was going on, she questioned as she walked slowly with her family out of the church. It all felt unreal; something huge had happened in the family and no one was able to say what it was exactly. Their bodies all huddled together in a swirling mass of black cloth reflected back the emptiness and the big hole she felt inside.

As soon as they got home Abigail headed furtively for the bottom of the garden. She wanted to be alone; she couldn't talk to her parents, brother or sister about what she felt right now. Everything was confusing, everything. She sat down in the dust, and her hands automatically started to scrape at the earth. Dust started to rise ever so slightly and she watched it, mesmerized by its liveliness compared to Aunt Robin's limp hand and hair. It seemed to permeate her being. She wanted a shroud of dust to smother her, envelop her, so the confusion she felt inside would be lost. Abigail scraped intensely now, her hands digging like an aardvark desperate for food. Her small hands gathered awkwardly the loosed red talcum and she threw it up violently in an effort to numb her senses. It formed a red cape that slowly descended, covering her black funeral clothes in smudges that grew as she rubbed at them.

She heard the echoes of African children off in the distance and she wondered if Zukah was there. They were laughing, a sound that bubbled over the dry wind and then burst in lightness. What was there to laugh about with all this seriousness in the air now that Aunt Robin was gone? Sweet sweet Zukah, he knew that this was a strange world, too. He'd always seemed to be the only other person that really understood her, him and Aunt Robin. She felt submerged in a vortex; a dark cavernous vortex where there were rules all around her but no one fully explained what the rules were, or why they were there in the first place.

She was reminded of the feeling again that the rest of the world wasn't like her world, but how would she know? No one seemed to think there was anything wrong with this world; but she felt it in her belly. She felt the fear. It burned unspoken on people's tongues. Their words came out quickly, like flowing silver, but there was little substance. Everyone seemed to pretend to be talking. They talked about small things like the car they had been wait-listed for, or what would happen on the weekend. No one talked about the tension in the air. No one breathed a word about why a black man could not sit down at the dinner table, or why Zukah could not come to her house for a visit. This was the stuff she wanted to know about. She never heard anyone explain why all the servants were black, and why there were servants anyway. Surely everyone had their own house to clean and their own family to raise. Why were the black people spending so much time doing the white people's jobs? If she could have conversations about these things, with real explanations, then she felt she could rise above the confusion. Robin and Zukah were the only people she felt comfortable talking to; and who explained things. Her parents were too busy helping all the needy people, and Samantha and Stephen didn't think about the things she did.

Why did Aunt Robin leave me? she thought. *She knew how much I needed her; why did she just go like that? I didn't even say goodbye,* Abigail thought angrily. It didn't feel right to be angry with Aunt Robin but she couldn't help it. Maybe the dust would take away the anger. She scraped her hand frantically across the red earth again, her nails digging in deeper, her hands clawing the earth with intensity. Then, holding on tightly to the red chalky substance barely contained in her small hand, Abigail threw her hand up quickly. With her small frame swaying chaotically she released it into the air again. As it descended, she pushed her head into the thickest cloud, hoping this time it would take away her ability to think. Take away the feelings of seeing Aunt Robin inert in that wooden box, her hair limp and mouth gaping. She breathed in heavily, praying that the dust would take away her thoughts. She held her breath, scared to release it in case the thoughts were still there.

Suddenly she started to cough uncontrollably. *This, maybe, will take away the horrible thoughts*, she thought. However when the coughing finally stopped, the confusion and fear sat inside like a boulder, as if they were taking up residence now that Aunt Robin had gone.

It was all too much; she hated even thinking about her thinking. *I will go and see the frogs at the river*, she thought. She got up abruptly and then stealthily headed toward the front gate, shoulders stooped low so she wouldn't be detected. Her mother was likely inside cooking dinner now; from the kitchen window she wouldn't be able to see Abigail heading into the bush across the road. Mom didn't like her going into the bush alone; "Anything can happen in the bush," she would say. What did she mean— what was "anything"? She never explained, so how would Abigail know? More confusion; her head felt plugged with it at times. She imagined all the unanswered questions just sitting there in her brain like dung beetle balls, and the more questions she added the less clearly she could think. Without Aunt Robin now to help clear some of the questions maybe she would have to see a doctor, and ask him how she could get the questions removed so she could concentrate at school. It was a frightening thought. *But maybe it's what I'll have to do someday,* she concluded.

Abigail tiptoed over the small granite stones on the driveway. She could feel them rubbing into tender places on her feet through the thin soles on her shoes. She liked the sensation: it felt like big thumbs massaging into inner crevices in her feet. Part of her wanted to take off her shoes and feel the stones between her toes, cooling her hot, clammy skin with their fresh cool surface. How come stones didn't heat up like the land, she wondered? Soon she was at the gate; she gingerly pulled up the metal latch, trying to avoid the clunk that her mother's ears were highly attuned to. Just as she lowered it, Bessie, the dog next door, started to bark, further muffling the soft metal sound.

Abigail darted over the road, and moved to the snaking red path that was visible below the tall bush grasses. They joined in an arc at the top of their stems. She relished bushwhacking, feeling the dry grasses on her body. Nature was with her, part of her, caressing her, befriending her in some way. She liked that feeling. Aunt Robin and Dad liked to bushwhack too. Sundays were her favorite day, when her brother, sister and her Dad, along with the dogs, would climb into the beat-up old saloon and head out. It was always after church so she would get restless sitting in the pews, but soon the time would come and they were all immersed in the wild African bush of Dombo-shawa.

Just up ahead Abigail saw a black head moving toward her. She couldn't see his body because of the grass but his head was erect. Suddenly his full body emerged, dressed in white clothes that told the world he was a helper for someone. His eyes bulged out of his head; the whites of his eyes were a bright white next to the molten chocolate color. The edges were creased as if he was in permanent laughter, but there was a grimace around his mouth that told a more serious story. "Good afternoon, Miss Abigail. Where are you going?"

"To the river, Mr. Josef."

He nodded his head in deference to her. He liked this girl; she seemed different from the other white girls. Her curiosity about nature was like the Africans'; he could see in her eyes a curiosity that permeated her being. His eyes took in the red brown smudges all over her black clothes. Africa was shrouding her with a cloak, he mused. Her hair, a sparkling mix of corn and gold, hung straight barely to her shoulders. He admired its texture. He had never touched a white person's hair but he imagined his fingers would have slid over it like wet, smooth grass. "What do you see at the river, Miss Abigail?"

"Frogs, Josef, haven't you seen the frogs? My aunt Robin died, Josef," she said, looking down at the path. "I'm scared about losing her."

"Oh, Miss Abigail, I am so sorry, I never met your aunt. Sorry, Miss Abigail sorry sorry, your heart is heavy I can feel it."

"Yes, Josef, my heart is attacked and there are so many questions in my mind, soon I don't know if my head can take any more questions."

"Ah, Miss Abigail, it is a strange world with so few answers for us all."

She drifted off, looking ahead and thinking of Aunt Robin. He had replied as Aunt Robin would have done. She remembered all the questions she had asked Aunt Robin. Her aunt never seemed to tire of hearing yet another. Her responses said, "I see your world and how hard it is for you." She would always say, "You are a wise one beyond your years! This will help you in life to hold firm." What did she mean, "hold firm?" Was that what she was doing now?

"Uh Miss Abigail I must go. Be careful now and I will send a prayer for your heart, Miss Abigail."

Abigail startled; lost in memories, she had momentarily forgotten Josef's presence. "Yes Josef, thank you Josef, and where is Zukah, Josef?"

"He just arrived; he is with his friends tonight. He will stay one more week before he goes back to the tribal trust lands."

He saw her heart deflate. Her mouth got tight and she pursed her lips. He knew they liked each other like a brother and sister. He would often find her at his quarters in the back garden kneeling down, and the two of them digging for termites with broken off sticks. Josef knew her parents realized they were friends, but he also knew that they shouldn't be seen playing together, that somehow he had to shield them both from the neighbors. He would tell them often to move closer to his dwelling's walls. Sometimes he got angry with them; he could tell they wondered why. The termites weren't there, why did they have to move over there, they would ask, and what was the big deal? A deep frown would push his son's eyes closer together and he would scowl. He hated this fear that he felt; he hated this country for shaming people. Shaming him in front of his son, shaming these children for digging for ants in full view of the neighbor. He hated a country also that had taken away his way of life; his people could no longer live on their land in the country. The government had given them small dry parcels of land, and so like most Africans he had had to get a job. Working for white people was demeaning. Every day he worked hard, but for what gain for him and his family? His white boss was happy, and his family was taken care of, but what about food for his own family? His pay was too small, and he imagined his children's bellies were often hungry because he was not there to help in the fields.

With Zukah's and Abigail's friendship, he knew he played a part in a racist ritual; but he was scared. Scared for his son's safety, scared of losing his job, scared of what people would say if they found out a black boy and a white girl had formed a friendship, even at the innocent ages of ten and twelve. A friendship as natural as the wind that caressed the land, he thought. A flowing effortless friendship built on bedrock of mutual curiosity. Josef could see their spirits merging, and nature submerging them in a world of intrigue. He remembered some of their questions: What happened to the lizard's tail—did someone bite it off? Would it grow back? Why do the termites go in a line? Is there a leader and where are they leading them? Why would the snake regurgitate the frog? Surely it was hungry; otherwise it wouldn't have tried to eat the frog. Josef had told Zukah some of these things and he in turn shared it with Abigail. When she had the answers a smile would come across her face and her spirit sighed. Yes, he liked this girl a lot.

"I need to go to work, Abigail. Enjoy the frogs! There are some buried in the river sand. If you are quiet they sometimes crawl out before the sun is going down." He smiled at her. "Also watch out for the big bullfrog; he is a big spirit."

She felt safe with him; he looked at her slowly as if he had taken the time to see her. What if she'd had Josef for a father, she wondered, would she still have these dung beetle balls in her brain? "Tell Zukah I'll see him at sunset tomorrow by your home, will you tell him that?" she pleaded, her voice pitching a little higher with an intense tone.

"Yes, Abigail, I will tell him. You will see him tomorrow evening."

Abigail hurried down the path. She knew if she was more than half an hour her mother would start calling her for dinner, and she would be found out. The path curved back and forth. She liked that; one couldn't see far in front, so each corner was a discovery. The ground was hard and dry; there were cracks in the red earth crust. The cracks showed a deeper red soil underneath. *How red does the soil get?* she thought. *Is it the color of blood near the bottom? Aunt Robin could answer my question, or she would know where to find an answer.* The image of Aunt Robin's mouth gaping open flashed in Abigail's mind and she felt her eyes get teary. Quickly she wiped them and hurried down the path.

The river appeared in her view around the next corner. It had shrunk since the last time she had seen it. It was slower moving; but still it had the calming burbling sound that she liked as it slipped over the rocks. On the bank she could see the mark where it had caressed the land with its moisture, and now it was hardening under the harsh African sun. She looked carefully onto the bank and noticed, about two meters away, a bullfrog standing still, like a rigid statue. His eyes took in her presence and slowly he blinked. His eyes were beady glistening marbles, in a head and body of camouflage green and mottled brown. His neck was dry red, as if the earth had masked and wrinkled him; but the rest of his body was still, moist and slimy from the river. He was fat, she thought; he must have been catching a lot of flies lately. He scared her and fascinated her at the same time. She looked closer, careful not to scare him with any movement from her body. He seemed to be focused on her, his eyes glazed and still. Josef had said he was a big spirit. Just then her heart started to beat louder; she looked at the bullfrog again and felt menaced by his gaze. *I better go,* she said internally.

Her legs scurried down the path, whose corners appeared threatening now, and she wished she could see in front. She burst out of the bush and waited impatiently for a car to come down the hill, focusing on its red lumbering shape careening ahead. The next thing she saw was a small white dog bunched under the back tire of the car. The dog was yelping, its whole form dragged slowly by the momentum of the screeching back wheel. Abigail dashed across the road after the car and screamed, but no one seemed to hear her. The car suddenly came to a halt and an elderly woman got out quickly, looking bewildered and shaken. Her hair was light lavender grey, and her eyes pale green orbs in her wrinkle-filled face. She wore a cream shirt and pants with a floral scarf loosely tied around her neck. Her hands were trembling. Immediately she bent down and gently pulled the small dog out onto the dirt pavement next to the street. The dog jerked and let out a muffled yelp again. Both could see that its back had virtually collapsed, and its legs were sprawled out next to its body like octopus tentacles. Abigail sat down hurriedly next to the dog and starting to stroke its head and neck. Its white coat was red in places with dirt, and it had thistles caught up in its fir. Its yelp now was reduced to a sickly whimper. Tears rolled down Abigail's face, dropping onto the dog's neck in hot drops. She kept stroking its head and neck, oblivious now of the elderly woman. They both knew instinctively the dog wouldn't survive, but Abigail wanted to soothe it, love it in its last moments. She kept stroking and stroking, while its whole body lay limp on the pavement. As she kept stroking, she noticed tendrils of wispy smoke that covered her hand, and covered the dog's body at the same time. The smoke seemed to follow her hand, moving back and forth across the dog's head and neck. The smoke was alive, bouncing up and down as it followed her stroke. She felt a wave of comfort, and then another soul-soothing wave. Mesmerized, she continued to stroke the limp form, unaware of the elderly woman crouching over her. The smoke entranced her; she lost track of time as she watched it zealously. Next the dog shuddered and its whole body and neck went limp; its eyes rolled back. Abigail collapsed over its body.

"He's died," she heard above her. "Oh that's terrible! I didn't even see him on the road." The woman bent over and touched the dog's head.

Abigail's eyes welled up and met the woman's gaze. She whispered, "He's died, the little dog has died and we don't know where he belongs, I didn't even see him run across the road. I just saw him being dragged by your tire, oh it's terrible. Did you see the smoke comforting him before he left?"

"What smoke? I didn't see any smoke. I'm not sure what you mean?" she looked quizzically at the dog, taking in his dead form once more.

"As I was stroking his neck this smoke followed my hand; it was trying to comfort the dog and me."

The elderly woman shook her head. "Look, this is terrible. I need to take him down to the vet to see if they recognize him and hopefully locate his owner. Have you seen this dog around here before?" she said, breathlessly stooped over his lifeless form with her hands starting to shake.

"No, the dog's not from here," Abigail replied, feeling puzzled and saddened at the same time.

"Could you put him in the boot of my car? I'm sorry, I don't know your name?"

"Abigail, I'm Abigail."

Abigail lifted up the lifeless form and noted the smoke had disappeared. She cradled him gently as she carried him. She shook her head as if it was all too much to take in, too much to absorb. Carefully she placed him in the boot of the car on a furry blanket; a little blood dripped out of his mouth.

"Oh I'm sorry Abigail, I must go, sorry that you had to see such a terrible thing today, am so sorry for this poor animal. I'm leaving town tomorrow so I must go; otherwise I would talk to your parents. Please take care, I am so, so sorry." She put her arm around her gently. Then she opened up the driver's door and soon the car started moving down the road.

Abigail stared for what seemed like ages. She saw the screech marks on the road, she remembered the dog's whimpering, but she could not stop fixating on the smoke. It was a terrible moment in her life, just like this morning, but somehow there was something comforting her, something soothing her, something letting her know that it would be OK, that she would be OK, that it was meant to be in some way. *How come the lady couldn't see the smoke?* she inquired to herself. *It was all over my hand and my arm.* Up and down, up and down it had moved, following each stroke like an obedient shadow.

Next moment she was pulling back the latch on the metal gate. She forgot about the clunk and raced up the driveway. Her mother was on the front steps looking annoyed. She had her apron on and her stance was matronly. Abigail knew she was in trouble.

"Where have you been, Abigail?" she bellowed sternly, her hands firmly attached to her slim hips. Abigail knew she was in big trouble when her mother's hands were in that position. Her mother was often anxious, but rarely angry. Abigail knew she was getting the spillover from the difficult day the family had had at Aunt Robin's funeral. When her mother was angry, she definitely looked older; her taut mouth, her wrinkled forehead, and her piercing blue eyes visible, only through narrowed slits, gave away her emotion.

"I saw a dog killed just opposite our driveway, it just happened now, right now, the dog died, an elderly woman ran over it, oh Mom it was so sad," the child cried out.

Her mother's demeanor changed in an instant. "Oh, Abigail, I am sorry, sweetie. That's awful! I can't believe we didn't hear it. Where is the dog now?"

"She took it in the car. It died next to me. Oh Mom, it was terrible," she heaved.

"What sort of a dog, Abigail? Was it a neighbor's dog?"

"No, I've never seen the dog before. It was a little white dog. It was awful. Its back was broken and it died as I was stroking it. Its body just jerked and then it died. I knew it was going to die, I just knew it, I wanted to save the dog but I couldn't," she heaved again.

Her mother put her arms around her and held her while she cried. Sinking her whole weight into her mother's body, she felt the warmth again that she had felt in the morning at church. She stayed for a long time until her mother started to shuffle a bit. "It's dinner time, Abigail; we need to tell the rest of the family what happened."

"OK, Mom, you can tell; I just don't feel like talking that much right now."

"OK, sweetie, it has been a terrible terrible day. Let's have some dinner to get some strength."

Abigail could feel another dung beetle ball move from her ears into her brain as she was hugging her mother. This was a big one. *How can I explain the smoke, and the feeling from the smoke, and the fact that the elderly woman couldn't see it?* She panicked inside. *Soon I won't be able to think for myself with all these dung beetle balls. What if the doctor can't get them out?*

Abigail knew the dog and smoke experience was a big event in her life; something important had just happened. It wasn't just the death of the dog and the funeral of Aunt Robin; something else had happened, and she didn't know quite what it was or how to describe it. Who could she talk to and get an answer? It was strange it happened on the same day as Aunt Robin's funeral. Who could she ask now that Aunt Robin was gone? Her parents were always busy with the stuff of their lives. There were always important events going on, politics, the government, what was happening in their jobs and how the children were doing at school. The questions in her house were always pointed to serious topics. There wasn't time to explore something, especially something vague and half-cooked.

Abigail was different; she wanted to explore and find out about things. She didn't have these firm opinions like her family. She was the youngest so she wasn't sure if this would change as she got older. She knew her family got irritated by her questions at times. It was if they were internally rolling their eyes. She could sense their thought, *Oh, here we go again.* Her father called her the "family philosopher"; it was meant to be funny and the family always laughed when he said it, but Abigail found it hurtful. She got the feeling that asking questions was bad for some reason, or maybe it was her type of questions; she wasn't sure. Samantha and Stephen could ask questions and it didn't get the same response—how come hers did? That was one of the biggest dung beetle balls in her brain, one that kept getting added to. It was her biggest question: *Why shouldn't I be asking questions?* She hadn't asked questions in a while, she felt, but tonight she would have to ask. *I can't help it,* she decided. *This is too big to keep inside.*

"Dinner's ready," her mother yelled down the corridor. Her voice dropped to a whisper as she turned to Abigail, frozen on her bed. "I've told everyone about the dog accident, and they know you don't want to talk about it."

"OK, Mom."

Abigail took her usual chair but positioned it out from the table a bit so everyone could see her clearly. While she waited, her heart fluttered a little.

She felt rocked still from Aunt Robin's funeral, the dog's death, and also the smoke on her hand and arm. She put her feet firmly on the floor, trying to find her ground. *I'll need to get some answers tonight,* she affirmed desperately. Just then her father and brother sat down. She looked at their faces, trying to gauge whether they were in the mood for her questions. Stephen's face looked drained and so did her father's. Stephen's striped green and white shirt hung off his shoulders loosely, making them look bigger. He had pushed his sandy hair back and so the scar from his rugby game was visible. *It's still quite deep,* Abigail thought. She looked at her father's face again. *He looks really tired,* she thought, but hopefully not too tired for her questions.

His eyes were fixated on the food on the table, and he started to play with his knife and fork in anticipation. Her father looked over to her eventually, his blue eyes fixed on hers, and said in a low voice, "Today was a very tough day for you, Abigail, and for all of us." He was such a big man in her eyes. His shoulders were wide and he walked with his head held high as if he had stuff to be proud about. He had a lot of brown hair and played with it often, pushing it back to a position he liked only to have it flop down like a visor over his eyes. It was as if he knew his hair was an asset and unconsciously drew attention to it. Although his mouth was tight, a grin was never far away. He was both light and heavy, Abigail thought, serious and funny; he attracted people like ants to sticky jam. She felt close to him; but his ideas were big ideas and it was hard to have her ideas stand next to his. She wished she had different ideas; then she could feel more comfortable around her father.

"I know," she clipped, pushing her chair further away from the table and pulling her hair into a ponytail, so somehow she would seem older. Her father leaned forward while Stephen grimaced and looked away from her. Abigail panicked inside, but she spat out, "When I was stroking the white dog that died, smoke followed my hand and was all over my arm. What do you think it means?" There. She got it out. She felt relief and desperation now for the answer.

At the same moment, her mother and Samantha walked in with the food. Everyone had heard her question. "What sort of question is that?" Samantha sneered.

Abigail winced inside. The scar got deeper, and she felt the tug at it, more hurt attaching to suppressed hurt.

"Come on, Samantha." Their father shook his head disapprovingly at Abigail's sister. "Give your sister a chance to explain herself: Abigail, what do you mean? Maybe you could describe it to us." He saw the pained grimace on Abigail's face and sensed her retreating. She worried him. She was so sensitive, so attuned to everyone and everything, he worried how she would get by in the business world, or any fast-paced environment. It wasn't that she wasn't bright; she was bright all right. He had discussed this numerous times with Jackie, his wife, and they both agreed that she was too deep for the everyday world.

At times he thought she questioned the strangest things. Though he liked some of her questions, it was hard to make time for them along with the needs of the other children. There was never a quick explanation; sometimes it took a long time just to understand the question. She must be struggling without Robin. He recalled how close they were, and the pleasure he used to feel seeing them coming up the drive together after a walk in the bush. His sister had a way of reaching Abigail that he found hard to mimic. *I will have to try harder now that she's gone.* It was hard to believe she was dead; then he remembered the coldness of her limp hand and a shudder went through his body.

"Well," Abigail said tentatively, with her foot jumping, hoping she would get the right words. She remembered she had left out the smoke's wispiness. "When I was comforting the dog that died, some wispy smoke moved over my arm, hand and the dog's neck; and it helped me a lot." *Whew!* she said inside. *I got the words.* Her foot stopped. Quickly she looked up for the family's reaction and despair washed over her. Her brother did an eye roll and turned his chair further away from her, and Samantha with her tawny straight hair and wild green eyes had disdain all over her face. Abigail dared to look at her parents. Her mother had that worried look again; and her father looked like he was feeling sorry for her. Her father cleared his throat.

"Abigail, there must have been a fire in the distance; you forgot to tell us that detail," he said in a matter-of-fact way, trying to ground her story in reality.

She was desperate now, desperate to save face and to keep her mind from being clogged up further with yet another dung beetle ball. Soon she wasn't going to be able to think; so it was critical she got an answer to this question. "There was no fire, this wasn't smoke from a fire, this was smoke over the dog's neck, my hand and arm. It felt comforting for some reason. I don't know why." Her foot started bouncing again.

Her mother started dishing out the steaming shepherd's pie, putting a dollop on each plate and handing it over impatiently. Stephen barked out, "I don't get you, Abigail," looking angry and irritated.

"Don't get angry at your sister," piped in their mother, banging the spoon noticeably on each plate to release her tension.

Samantha's body was moving back and forth. "There's something wrong with your brain, Abigail," she spurted, leaning over to put peas on her plate.

Abigail leaped up and pushed her plate away. "I'm sick of this family!" She pulled down her black top and ran toward her bedroom, desperate to lock the door and shield herself from all this cruelty.

Her mother followed her hurriedly, her shoulders hunched in guilt for not protecting her, only to be met by a slammed door. "Open the door, Abigail," she pleaded. "Everyone is just tired; we had a hard day, all of us, at Robin's funeral." She leaned against the door and listened for any movement.

"They're tired of me and my questions; that's what they're tired of. I just won't talk to anyone anymore," Abigail sputtered through hot tears. "No one understands me, only Auntie Robin and she's dead, and Zukah," she wailed inconsolably.

Jackie leaned against the door, feeling fatigued by it all. It was hard to respond because her daughter had often put her finger on major problems. However, there were so many problems, and this was one more to add to her heavy shoulders. Some of those problems were at the clinic where she worked as a counselor. They had lost more staff lately. Whites were leaving the country in droves. Ever since the bombing in the downtown Salisbury hotel, many whites had started to send out immigration papers to Australia, Canada, Britain, and New Zealand. They were going wherever they could get through the gates. Three people had recently resigned at work—there were plenty of black people out of work but they needed to be trained; and who was freed up to train them? The whites needed to release the colonial reins and support a full black government; not this quasi power shift of a biracial government when there was no history of sharing power. *Man, this is such a difficult country to live in at times!* She loved the natural world, the people and the wildness; but everything felt so unstable, even compared to Northern Ireland, where they had immigrated from fifteen years ago. She often wondered if this was the right country to bring up their children, with all its political problems.

Moments had passed, and she had forgotten about Abigail upset inside her room. A heavy silence filled the air. What could she say that would get the girl to open the door and talk?

"Abigail, why don't I get your dinner and we'll have ours together in your room—then I can hear all about the dog and the smoke."

"It's wispy smoke," Abigail responded quickly. She sounded desperate to be understood.

Jackie stiffened but contained her response. "I mean your wispy smoke and the little dog that died. I'll go and get our dinner—OK?"

"OK," Abigail sniffled softly.

Jackie went back to the dinner table feeling both relieved and concerned about Abigail. She picked up Abigail's plate and started to scoop peas onto the side. "That was a really hurtful thing to say, Samantha, and you too, Stephen. You know she's sensitive; she just wanted to ask a question, that's all."

"Her questions are so weird, Mom. Where does she get them?" Samantha defended herself, twirling hair between her fingers.

"She's irritating," Stephen coughed back with no remorse in his voice. "I can't help getting irritated at her. Why can't she talk like a normal person? I know she saw a dog die, but why this other stuff?"

"She's your sister and she feels hurt now. Look, we all went to Auntie Robin's funeral today, and it was tough on all of us. On top of that Abigail saw a dog die in an accident right outside our house. Clearly it's too much for her all in one day. Just try a little harder, please, both of you." Jackie grabbed both plates and forks in her hand.

Bill looked up at her. "Can you manage, Jackie? Will she let you in?"

She sighed, "Yes, she's waiting for me." Her neck stiffened at the thought of the conversation that was ahead of her.

Abigail had unlocked the door. Jackie found her sitting on a Hessian carpet on the floor, staring trance-like out the window at the dying sunset. She felt the girl recoil and knew she needed to manage her responses well. "OK, Abigail, tell me what you saw—I'm all ears," she said, shuffling her body back and forth.

"You don't really want to hear my story, Mom; I can tell you're not interested," Abigail muttered in resigned tones. "You feel sorry for me— that's why you're here. I hate it when people feel sorry for me." The room echoed with the odd click of the child picking at her nails.

Jackie put a plate in front of Abigail, and then sat down on a high-backed straw chair opposite her daughter. Internally she sighed, but she tried not to show it. *How on earth am I going to tackle this one?* she thought. *This is the weirdest topic yet.* She wondered if this could be a result of her friendship with Zukah, maybe getting overly exposed to Shona spiritual customs. *Maybe we need to monitor her contact with that African boy.* She hoped this wasn't a sign that the topics would get increasingly strange in the future. She placed her dinner on her lap but ignored it for now, using all her energy to muster a response for the coming dialogue.

"I am here because I care about you, Abigail. Now tell me what happened when you were comforting the poor dog." She breathed in heavily, hoping to create some space in her mind for this strange tale.

Abigail, part relieved but still hurt, rubbed her black skirt now so the smudges of dust started to lighten as they grew tentacles. Her thin brown legs with soft blonde hair looked vulnerable, her whole body fragile. She started out softly: "Well, I saw the dog being dragged by the back tire, and there was nothing I could do. I screamed and then the car stopped. This old lady got out, just like I told you. She pulled the dog out and it was limp; its back was broken, I think. It was just whimpering. It was terrible. I thought it was going to die, so I wanted to stroke it, to help it, then when I was stroking it this smoke passed over my hand and arm and its body. What seemed so weird was that it followed my hand back and forth. I don't know what it was, but it had this strange feeling with it, like everything was going to be OK."

"What do you think it was?" Jackie asked, making an effort to keep her tone measured. She felt some irritation that her dinner was getting cold but she knew now was not the time for any distraction; she sensed that her daughter needed all of her. Abigail stared into her mother's eyes intensely; her gaze revealed a pleading for acceptance, acceptance for who she was in the world.

"Well ..." she said, drawing it out while she mustered the courage to go on, her body starting to rock back and forth gently now. "I don't know," then added in a whisper, "but I know it was something strange."

"Uh-huh," murmured Jackie, pleased with how she was regulating her tone in spite of her daughter's intensity. She crouched over Abigail's body more, both to get closer to her, and to stretch out some of the tension building in her neck.

Abigail was twirling her black top into a spiral in her hand and her movements were getting more frantic. "I don't know, Mom, I just don't know. I just know it's something strange."

Jackie noticed that the more Abigail talked, the more a trance seemed to come over her, as if it had taken possession of her. *Tell me she's not becoming mentally ill; oh, please, God, don't let this be a first sign of schizophrenia.* Her body shuddered at the thought; she remembered the look on another mother's face when she'd brought her teenage son into the clinic for a mental health assessment. The mother had phoned in private earlier, distraught at the bizarre nature of her son's behavior. She spoke of finding him in a room talking to himself, barely noticing her presence, as if he had gone away somewhere and she couldn't get him back. When she arrived at the clinic with her son, he was disheveled, a white shirt hanging off his shoulders to reveal his pale flesh underneath, his jeans sliding down his torso. Jackie recalled the mother's face drowning in anguish, remembered wincing at her pain. The woman's eyes had looked haunted; as if she were experiencing her worst nightmare and she knew it was going to be lifelong. Her shoulders were doubled over and she looked fragile enough for a small gust of wind to push over. *Oh please God, please don't let my daughter have schizophrenia!*

"What did it feel like, Abigail?" she blurted, relieved that she had come out with an appropriate question. Jackie noticed relief wash over her daughter's face. The girl's mouth loosened and her piercing pale green eyes looked softer. The twirling of her top stopped momentarily, her finger under the fabric relaxed and folded over. Jackie noticed all of this—she felt scared and comforted at the same time.

"I felt calmed and scared by it. It felt like someone was there, but I was scared by seeing the smoke; I was scared I was going crazy."

Jackie shuddered internally, trying to contain the reaction on her face. Abigail saw the flash of fear in her eyes and her body startled a bit. She needed her mother to accept her; she wanted assurance that she wasn't going crazy, that someone could remove the dung beetle balls from her brain, and that people would understand her questions and answer them.

"What happened next, Abigail?" *Whew!* Jackie said internally. She knew she couldn't trust herself to comment, with her thoughts swept into the whirl-pool of fear that swam around and around in her mind. She saw Abigail look down, her shoulders collapsing.

Abigail had wanted assurance that she wouldn't get rejected this time, that her ideas would be validated. She knew her mother loved her, but she didn't feel fully understood by any family member. Her mother's anxiety got in the way of her hearing her. She felt her mother was always trying to calm things down, muffle reactions, keep things on an even keel. This felt a bit different, though.

"I came home quickly, didn't I; I don't know if the smoke followed me or not."

"Oh," said Jackie; it was all she could muster. *What in heaven's name does one say in response to that?*

"Is that all you can say, Mom, 'Oh'? What do you mean by 'Oh'?" Abigail looked at her as accusingly as a prosecutor. Jackie realized that it was her support of her daughter that was on trial.

"Well," Jackie hesitated, "it's, uh, it uh, just, I thought the smoke would have followed you home, that's all." She clutched her cold dinner plate with intensity.

Abigail softened. "Well, it might have, Mom; I just don't know, do I?"

"I suppose you don't. How would you know, anyway?" *My goodness,* thought Jackie, *this is one of the most bizarre conversations I have ever had.* She was troubled and impressed at how she was getting into the groove of it all. Her head was feeling light, dizzy. She felt as if she were being trans-ported to some strange new world in a time machine with her daughter.

"Well," Abigail offered, "I could look out the window and see if I can see the smoke now," assuming that would somehow comfort her mother and lower her anxiety.

"Why don't you do that, Abigail; and I need to eat some dinner before I faint." Jackie slumped in the chair.

Abigail leaped up, her spindly brown legs popping out of her black skirt like two ochre table legs, her skirt all puffed up and ill-shapen as if a gust of wind had blown inside. She pulled at her lemon yellow curtain, and pushed against the oak desk that held all of her pens and crayons in an African wooden holder. She stared out of the window, intent on uncovering this mystery before her, feeling stronger now that she had her mother by her side. She looked out over the garden with its browning kikuyu lawn, and the vague shape of the swimming pool off in the distance. It was hard to see anything in the sun's dying embers of burnt orange with vermillion streaks, swallowed into the night sky. Jackie saw Abigail's eyes narrowing, as if her vision needed to be altered in some way to see this strange phenomenon. There was no doubt in Jackie's mind that she had witnessed something. Her daughter was telling her truth; that much was certain. She stared at the cold shepherd's pie that looked inert and limp on her plate and spooned in a mouthful. It seemed to help ground her in this moment of madness. The texture of the meat between her teeth gave some substance to her thoughts. She felt as if she were holding onto a thin metal pole in a hurricane of ethereal wind.

"Do you see anything Abigail, any smoke?" Thank goodness Bill wasn't here; he would have been mortified that she was feeding into their daughter's madness. *"We have to keep the girl anchored,"* he would say over and over again. *How in the hell do we do that right now?* Jackie mentally demanded in response to the memory of her husband's words. *Oh sure, great idea, Bill, but how do we do it?* He was good at quick fix ideas, but she was the one who had the burden of figuring out the methods. Jackie knew intuitively that in this moment, her daughter needed to feel she was holding her hand as she stared into the abyss. This was not a moment to challenge her reality, or she sensed that the girl could retreat for weeks, and then this madness could really get a hold.

"No, nooo, I don't think so," Abigail said, narrowing her eyes even more.

"What do you mean, you don't think so?" Jackie snapped. This was all too much and she threw another forkload of shepherd's pie into her mouth. "You either see it or you don't," she mumbled through the food. Should she be relieved that this smoke apparently hadn't followed her daughter home, or should she be afraid that it had and was going undetected? *God, I am losing my grip.* Jackie ground her teeth over the meat in the pie, tasting nothing but the acid of the intense stress rising in her.

"Don't shout at me, Mom. I'm trying to see it," Abigail wailed in a high-pitched tone. Just then her Dad knocked on the door.

"Abigail, can I come in?" He moved through the door, hesitating for a moment. He pushed his fringe back, his eyes looking quizzical under the mass of hair. His knees creaked at the effort to lower his body onto the bed. Jackie could feel his impatience. She tried to catch his eye, but he was focused on his daughter's frame leaning up against the window looking for something.

"What are you looking for, Abigail?" he ventured cautiously.

"The smoke, of course Dad. I'm seeing if it followed me." She kept her eyes glued up ahead, not sensing the tension in her father, nor the frantic gestures between her parents.

Bill glared at his wife, his body in shock; he felt his eyes burn. *She may be in the mental health field, but this is out of control. Abigail has never talked like this before.* He shook his head unconsciously.

"Dad, can Mom and I go tomorrow to look for the smoke where the dog died?" she pleaded, knowing how profound his approval would be.

"Yah," he muttered barely audibly, looking over at her and then gazing at the ground. "Eat up, Abigail. I'm off for a walk. You'll feel better once you've had some dinner and changed out of your black clothes." He had to believe that; maybe she was lightheaded and that was why she was seeing things. Dealing with two deaths in one day, it had obviously been too much for her, he reflected. He left hurriedly, shouldering his concern like a heavy, invisible backpack as he passed through the door.

"Yes, eat up dear, and you better jump into the bath to get rid of all that dust." Jackie stood up slowly. She moved gingerly toward the door; feeling off balance, as if the earth had shifted under her. She sensed that she and her daughter had taken the first step in a long, long journey.

Chapter 2

Zukah was squeezed next to his father on the bus to Umtali. If the bus didn't die en route, Zukah anticipated he would be home in about three hours. It was such a quick visit. He was shocked and disappointed he didn't get to spend time with Abigail or say goodbye to his friends. His father insisted there was no time to waste as the funeral would happen soon, and he too was keen to get back quickly to the village after such tragic news.

It was overwhelming to hear about his uncle's death. Zukah couldn't drink in the news to any depth. The boy had spent more time with Uncle Temba than with his own father. His uncle had shown him how to herd the cattle, and to plow the land for the crops. Uncle Temba was like another father for Zukah. He'd treated him like a son, guiding him in the customs of the people. "Always remember, Zukah," he'd told him, "for the Shona people the spirits are with us every day. Our family is both the living and the dead. The *Mudzimu* (ancestral spirit) protects us and we heed their advice as they help our *rudzwi* (our kind) stay strong. Never turn your back on the spirits; they can punish us if we are not heeding their wisdom."

A visitor from their village at Umtali had knocked on his father's door in the early morning. He was a tall man with soot-black skin that shone as if waxed with polish. His eyes were sunken and red, his shoulders stooped under the burden of the news he had to share. He said quietly, in a raspy voice, "Josef, quickly, you need to come back to the village. Temba has died. He was plowing the land and a cobra struck him. The people are not sure whether he had angered some spirits." Zukah cried out and his father fell down on the floor. "I have fallen on a spear," his father had said to the visitor. "My heart is bleeding for my brother." Zukah saw his his body rock with emotion as he kept repeating, "I have lost my brother."

"Aaayh," the visitor said, "Aaayh, we are with you, brother, in your sadness."

As quickly as the visitor had arrived, he was gone. Zukah, struck numb with grief, watched his father, still trembling, throw some clothes into a bag and prepare for their journey. "We will head out now, Zukah; I will tell Boss Smithers that I will be gone for four days for the funeral. Get your bags, Zukah. There is no time to waste; Uncle Temba's spirit is waiting for us."

Zukah followed his father to the kitchen door of the white household. He wondered how Mr. Smithers would treat his father, given he would be leaving his garden duties suddenly. Josef knocked loudly, and Mr. Smithers swung open the top part of the wooden door. Zukah thought the man looked both curious and irritated. His short brown hair was pasted to the side of his face; his khaki shirt was open, baring the golden hairs on his chest.

"Josef, what is happening?" he asked, knowing it was unusual to see Josef this early in the morning.

"Aah, Boss." Zukah watched his father bow his head and clasp his hands together in deference to his employer. "My brother has passed away. I need to go to the funeral. They are waiting for me."

Mr. Smithers peered over the door and saw the bag between him and Zukah, realizing that his departure was imminent. "I'm sorry about your brother, but we need you, Josef: the lawn needs cutting, we have lots of jobs in the garden … When can you be back?" his tone was clipped, to the point, his hawk-like eyes fixed on Josef's bags.

"Aah, boss, I need four days." Josef hung his head down again.

"Four days! Can't you come back earlier? Won't they bury him quickly? I need you here, Josef," his voice pressured as his hand gripped the half-door.

"Boss, the village, they need me. I have duties to perform, please, boss, it is my brother, my brother has gone." Josef started to rock again in an effort to contain himself, leaning up against Zukah as a way of holding on.

Smithers closed his eyes as if to shut out the apparition of a grown man in open mourning. He started to close the half-door. "OK, Josef, we'll see you on Tuesday morning. I'll tell Madam."

"Aah, thank you boss, thank you boss," he repeated bowing his whole body in gratitude.

As Zukah sat on the bus, he went over the events again in his mind: The early morning visitor with his red eyes and raspy voice, the terrible news about Uncle Temba. He kept thinking of the snake attacking his uncle's leg; then his uncle's large frame falling into the bush with a thud. His father bowing to Boss Smithers. He had not seen his father in mourning; he had not had a close relative die before. The grief for Uncle Temba felt frozen in his body, as if his heart had been dipped into the white boss' freezer with the meat, and it hadn't had time to thaw out.

He remembered Abigail's face when he met her on their way out as she was biking to school. He told her Uncle Temba had died and that they were leaving. He had never seen his white sister's face look so distraught before. Her eyes were really scared, he reflected. Scared of what? He recalled their quick conversation, trying to match the information she told him with the look on her face. "I'm sad for you Zukah; you loved Temba," she kept repeating. He recalled her telling him breathlessly that her auntie had died, the one she had talked about that visited from Canada. She didn't have to tell him she loved her auntie dearly; every time she'd repeated Auntie Robin's tales, light would come into her eyes, intensity into her voice. Why was his white sister so scared? He would understand her being sad, like he was right now, devastated and overwhelmed, but why the fear? He sensed her fear was as big as a mountain. *Isn't that weird we both lose a relative at the same time? Our worlds are so different, but our lives so similar.* The thought sat with him, made him uneasy. *Did I miss something my "white lily" was trying to tell me?* Soon the uneasy feeling submerged with other feelings churning inside him and left him with an overwhelming feeling of dread.

Zukah looked around him. The bus was full of black people; all he could see were clothed legs and black hands all around him. One man close by had a chicken in a basket at his feet. It was clucking and trying to push its beak through the grass slits all around it. Zukah watched its eyes, golden beady orbs darting here and there; he felt the chicken's nervous spirit fill in the gaps between the bodies. He wanted to free the chicken, take it out of the cage and throw it out of the dusty red window, release its spirit.

A river of sound enveloped him, voices ululating with the chicken. The confusion he felt was compounded by the noise. He did not understand his place in this society. His uncle's status as the village headman had given him special attention in the village, where Zukah was able to learn the importance of helping people through negotiation. He had a place in the village; he felt his roots deep in the African soil, and he felt secure in village life. Now that Uncle Temba had died, would his place in the village change? When he came to the city to see his father he felt mostly invisible. He moved furtively around the dominant white world. He knew that he needed to be hidden from the neighbors; his father had told him, "No African boy can be seen here without permission from a white boss, only servants can be on the white man's land." Seeing his father's humility in front of the white man confirmed his confusion. Where did his kind fit in outside of the village? What was his place in this world full of colored metal cars, big buildings and white people's noise? He didn't know, and his father's uncertainty of his own place in that world confirmed his suspicion that he didn't fit in. He had asked Uncle Temba and he always said, "Zukah, you have a big spirit. Your spirit cannot squeeze into a white man's cage. Always remember that, Zukah."

Slowly the bus lumbered out of the city. It was an old diesel bus and Zukah heard it groan under its heavy load of passengers, livestock, furniture, and bags; it sputtered every time it came to a stop. Every now and then the bus would lunge forward as if it had a quick burst of energy, and the passengers would let out a wail and grab onto anything they could reach. Zukah saw a young woman, bent like a willow tree in a strong wind, clutch a man's leg. The man smiled, she smiled back shyly, and then she straightened back to her full willowy height.

Zukah peered through the slits in the window that weren't smudged with dust. He saw the bush outside and a farmhouse way off in the distance. He felt his body sigh, sigh at the thought of being back in nature. He liked the stimulation of the city and seeing his friends, especially his "white lily," but that displaced feeling eventually built up and it was a struggle to ignore it. It was OK for his "white sister"; she belonged there, although her spirit was indigenous African. Somehow he couldn't imagine her in the tribal trust lands. He wondered why in many ways she was more indigenous than his city friends. Many of his city friends were working on farms on the outskirts of the urban areas; they seemed to have adapted. He felt they were a bit different from him now but he couldn't explain why. Maybe they weren't as peaceful, he thought, as peaceful as his friends in the village. *Perhaps they don't know their place in the city, all those white people telling them what to do all the time.*

The bus started to bounce up and down now that it had taken a turn onto a dirt road. Red dust swirled around the bus, following it like a shadow. Zukah stared at the dust, imagining it was the spirit of the ancestors, or maybe Uncle Temba's spirit guarding the people. It encompassed them like a shroud and then released into the sky like fading smoke—*back to where they came from*, he mused. Eventually the bus came to a stop and they descended.

Zukah and Josef walked slowly toward the village. His father's steps were somber, silent but resolute. The sun burned fiercely overhead, the heat drying the land, the air parched and thin. Zukah saw his father's grief nestled on his back; his back stooped over as if his sadness sat on it and forced it to bend. This was his father's only brother, so who would take his place in guiding Zukah, lead him through his initiation as a man, give him his place in the village? His father had explained to him many times that he could not stay in the village, he needed to earn money so the family could eat. Zukah had got used to it as Uncle Temba had taken over the paternal role, but now what would happen?

As they got closer to the village Josef and Zukah could hear the wailing and the drums; they quickened their pace on the thin dusty path. The dogs had heard their footsteps; one started to bark while another came running over, panting in the noonday heat. "Go," said Josef, sensing it was sniffing his bag for food.

The dog was thin, its ribs carved out clearly beneath its mottled, sinewy skin. Its nipples were enlarged. The dog had pups and was clearly desperate for food; perhaps it had traveled a long way, surmised Zukah, searching his bag. He pulled out a dry, half-eaten slice of bread. He looked at his father to get his approval; but he was too preoccupied to even notice. Zukah threw the slice onto the soft red dust. The dog gnashed at it in seconds; then licked its lips continually as if this was an appetizer and more was on its way. Zukah looked ahead and saw the men and woman collected outside his uncle's hut. His father rushed over, collapsing into his mother's arms. They rocked together, wailing. She clutched at his head, pulling it to her body, collapsing under the weight of grief.

"Aaay, aaay, Temba has gone, Temba has gone." Her pitch intensified every time she said her son's name.

"Temba, Temba," Josef cried out in response as if he were trying to will his brother back to life. Zukah saw his own mother approach his father, his baby brother secured tightly with a brown sheet on his mother's back, so only his right cheek was visible. Her hand reached out to her daughter who was crying, overwhelmed by the sadness all around her. Zukah loved his sister Della; she always brought over his food when the family got together to eat. She loved following him in the bush and always encouraged him to stop to stare at the creatures on their path. Her favorite was the giant millipede, or *chongololo*; just like his "white lily" Abigail. He took his sister's hand, and squeezed it tightly, trying to reassure her in this moment of confusion and grief for all in the village.

Men and women gathered around them, their bodies swaying with grief. They enfolded Zukah and his sister Della in their mass of vibrating flesh. He felt absorbed by the bodies. The air was tight, but he felt held, held by his people, held by their customs, held in this moment of tragedy.

The group eventually moved closer to the hut; then parted to make way for Josef and Zukah to enter the dwelling. Josef bowed his head and clutched at Zukah's hand. Josef placed a tooth of an animal in Zukah's palm and then pulled him through the narrow doorway. Other men followed behind, all solemnly bowing their heads to mark the importance of the event. At first Zukah could not see; he blinked and then blinked again, trying to make out the shapes in the dark, cold void in the hut. Soon shapes began to form: He saw Uncle Temba lying on a raised hard mud surface, straw under his body. His head was tilted back and his eyes were all white. Zukah screwed up his eyes, trying to recreate in his mind Uncle Temba's eyes, eyes that burst out of his face like beacons of molten hope. Zukah scanned the parts of his body not covered by a grey blanket and clothing and saw the dried blood on his shin; he looked more closely and saw some marks indicating the fangs of a snake. His father took his son's hand, and gestured to him to drop the animal tooth into a bowl close to his uncle's head. He had been told before about this custom: The tooth was *chema*, a ritual token indicating his respect and honor for his relative. As Zukah placed it carefully, the grief rose in him. He felt it like a river bursting through him, exploding his senses in sadness. He felt his body lean against his father's, like he was losing his ground. Josef then placed his token in the chema bowl and bowed over his brother's body, his tears splashing on his brother's shirt. Zukah watched them form—small splotches collecting on Uncle Temba's shirt. He watched the tears trickle down his uncle's neck and collect on the nape of his neck. It comforted Zukah, seeing his father's imprint on Uncle Temba.

Just then a quiet, distant voice started to make some sounds. The voice spoke slowly, each sound forming with intense effort, as if it were the last. At first Zukah thought the voice was emerging from Uncle Temba's mouth even though it sounded far, far away, but the dead man's mouth appeared frozen on his round face. Zukah heard the words echo as if a wind were trying to carry them. He had never heard a dead man talking before—he knew this was Uncle Temba's spirit. The sound both frightened and calmed Zukah. The boy shivered; he felt his uncle's spirit wash over his flesh like fresh rain. He clenched his father's hand more tightly.

Josef stood firm and alert, for he knew these would be precious words and he wanted to remember them for all time. "Josef, I am gone, you are my brother, we are always brothers. You will be headman, Josef, but be aware there is a snake in our village. The snake arranges an attack on the leg, but it affects the hearts and minds of our people. The people are not aware of the snake; he uses his charms to stay hidden, but we are brothers and we will protect our rudzwi. We are together." The voice sounded like it was dying out. Josef bent deeper over the body, inhaling the words into his core, but the next words were not addressed to him:

"Zukah, my spirit is by your side. I have taught you in the ways of our people. Do not forget our ways. You will live in both worlds. Like the life-giving baobab tree, you will stand tall and offer much to people in both worlds. But do not forget the roots of the tree: you are Shona. Do not be swayed by the ways of the white man, for he seduces us to forget who we are. Never forget, Zukah." As Zukah heard his name the second time the voice started to fade. He sensed the wind had swallowed his uncle's voice. Another enormous wave of sadness welled in him. Josef and Zukah stood there, hands clutching each other, frozen in time. Neither moved, their spirits suspended in anticipation of the voice returning, their bodies bent over the inert body of their relative like bulrushes protecting the water below. Zukah could hear the cries outside and the drumbeat mimicking the pain in the villagers' hearts. After a long time, he felt his father pull his hand; they both slowly moved out of the opening in the hut, leaving Temba lifeless behind them.

Zukah stood there detached and watched the villagers as they danced and sang in mourning. Bodies swaying rhythmically, their hearts appeared to beat as one. His mother and grandmother clutched onto his father, all rocking together, their hands on each other's back propping each other up. Zukah saw Temba's wife Nyala wiping her face repeatedly, smoothing the tears of sadness into her black skin. Her sinewy body was erect, standing firm in the soil, anchoring her two daughters on either side of her, but her spirit looked broken and her eyes reflected fear. Zukah noticed Temba's daughter Busi hanging her head down, seemingly unaware of the commotion around her, her legs folding over her knees like she had lost her ground. Her taller sister looked ahead, eyes sunken and glazed, her mouth open in confusion. Zukah felt his own pain reflected in her eyes.

Zukah felt alone. He knew his path had changed dramatically. He instinctively pushed his feet deeper into the earth, kicking up the hard crust. Loose red dust escaped under the pounding feet of the villagers. It swayed around the ankles of the dancers, caressing their feet with tendrils of red smoke before descending back to the earth. Zukah imagined it was Uncle Temba's spirit, rising and falling with his people. He felt his presence was there in the dust; he was dancing with the dancers, swaying with his people, he was with them in their dance of sadness. He felt soothed for a moment; he knew too that the people would feel comforted in the future with Uncle Temba as a Mudzimu.

After a while Zukah saw some men approach his father. One man pointed in the direction of the jacaranda tree on the edge of the village, away from the mud huts and cleared space. Some of the dancers noticed and their feet slowed down, even though the drumbeat continued to resound, carrying the spirits to a deeper place. Then the drummers responded, slowing down the beat, *boom, da boom.* Zukah felt the shift in the people; he felt their spirits descending back to earth, reinhabiting their bodies. A cloud of stillness hovered over them, holding them in that moment. Josef beckoned to Zukah to join him and slowly they walked together, leading the villagers in the direction of the jacaranda tree. Zukah saw four men go into Uncle Temba's hut. They were carrying between them two branches of a tree joined by some animal skin in the middle. Zukah wanted to watch but his father pulled at his hand to keep up with the procession. Soothing sounds emerged from the group, the murmur of the villagers' voices. Loosely formed Shona words drifted off their tongues in a low hum. Zukah turned his head around and saw the four men walking now alongside the group. They held the branches tightly, with Uncle Temba limply suspended by the animal skin, his legs hanging precariously, waving back and forth as if his body were still alive and performing a dance of its own.

As they neared the tree, Zukah's steps slowed. It stood there dominating the landscape, its lavender flowers delicately attached to form clusters of purple reaching into the sky, piercing the blue. It was the Queen of trees, thought Zukah, and the Baobab the King; it was so proud with its height and its unique splash of color among the earthy browns and greens of the land. In the shadow of the jacaranda tree there was an elongated hole. Zukah saw the moist red earth exposed. The red clay clung together in a smooth wall on either side of the hole. He could smell the sweat of the villagers all around him, a dry musk carried on a faint breeze. The men carrying Uncle Temba slowly moved him near the hole and lowered the branches. Suddenly his feet hit the earth, pushing his knees up as if his legs had come alive and he was about to get up and stand. Zukah's heart leaped—a flash of fantasy of his uncle stepping off the skin and walking toward him permeated his psyche. It dissipated quickly into the hot African air as soon as his Uncle was placed on the ground. He witnessed the limpness of his body, his stiff mouth and white eyes rolled back. His body sagged as if deflated; the flesh hung loosely like fabric to reveal the bone beneath.

He watched as the men took his uncle's limbs and, straddling the hole, lowered the body into the earth. The men's faces were somber, their grim expressions denoting the loss for the village. Zukah peered over the side and saw the body lie lifeless at the bottom of the hole. Josef nodded to the men, voicing his approval of the positioning of his brother's corpse, in the tradition of their rudzwi.

Next Josef stood at the top of the grave. "I call on my grandfather's spirit, Josiah, I call on the spirit of Dadirai my great-grandmother," and so the list continued as he named numerous relatives that had left for the spirit world. "Please welcome our beloved Temba, a spirit of many gifts, a man for the people. He has a lion's heart. Welcome our brother to you; let his spirit be at peace." The villagers let out "ayeeee, ayeeee. Let him be at peace, ayeeee, ayeeee, our Temba is at peace." The carriers placed a thick stick the length of the grave against Temba's body, and then angled it to reach to the top corner of the grave. Then slowly with branches they moved the soil onto the corpse. Zukah saw the moist earth falling onto Uncle Temba's white eyes and covering his neck, until only a cheek was exposed. Soon the thick red blanket of clay shrouded the cheek and all of his body. The stick poked through the soil, exposed to the elements. He remembered his father telling him that when someone dies a stick is placed in the grave, and pulled out after the soil has settled. This ensures that a passage is formed for the spirit, in the form of a caterpillar, to depart the grave and wander freely. His father had said that in time the family would then perform a kurova guva ceremony and call the spirit back to the family.

Zukah looked down again at the grave and the poking stick. *He is gone, my uncle is gone, he has gone to the spirit world, and he will turn into a caterpillar and wander the land.* Zukah quickly looked down to make sure his feet were not about to land on a caterpillar at that moment. He vowed to look for Uncle Temba's spirit in the months to come, searching the land for caterpillars that were arching their hairy bodies rhythmically over the dry land.

His heart heaved again with sadness. At that moment he felt a force press against his heart, like a piece of wood pushing up against it. He focused on it fully; the sensation was strange as he had never felt it before, then he felt his heart expanding and inflating with a presence. He breathed deeply, and deeply again. He sensed Uncle Temba was with him, in his body for that brief moment. He smiled quietly; his uncle was helping him to suspend his grief, holding his heart with his spirit. Zukah bowed his head in deference; perhaps he would be able to manage the tumultuous change after all.

Chapter 3

Bill lay in bed, his eyes fixated on the ceiling, desperately trying to take in the day. He couldn't stop thinking about his sister; the finality of seeing her in the coffin had unhinged him. It was too big a shock. He could feel his body repel the image; he remembered picking up her hand; his impulse had been to shake it violently to life. He couldn't imagine living in a world without his sister. Family memories in Northern Ireland flashed before him: their snow fights, her selling her candies to him. He remembered her standing up for him with their father numerous times, protecting him from his father's wrath. Her family piano recitals, how proud she was to play the piano, her music transporting them all. *Imagine poor Peter,* he thought. Having to go back to Canada with her body and bury her there. How was Peter going to cope? He had encouraged him to stay for a while, but Peter made it clear he wanted to return on the soonest flight out. Now Bill couldn't even visit Robin at her graveside to talk to her. There was too much going on. He couldn't deal with his sister's death right now. It was all too much, too many problems, so much instability; no, he couldn't think of Robin right now, it was all too much.

The conversation with Abigail had unnerved him. What a day for it to happen. Robin's funeral and the dog accident was clearly too much for her in one day. It must have unhinged her, he concluded. He felt like he was about to lose it in her bedroom; the walk was essential to retreat from an angry outburst. Jackie was cool when he came to bed and didn't want to discuss anything. He wanted assurance from her that everything was all right with the family; but Jackie's behavior told him something different. He always felt unsettled when Jackie retreated into a shell. It was the part of her that he found the most challenging. He was a "what you see is what you get" type, with no secrets brewing under the surface. He would have just spoken about whatever was troubling him.

Jackie was different. He relied on her emotional state as a gauge of how the whole family was doing, so her retreat triggered his anxiety. He had never questioned Abigail's mental state before, but this last set of questions had thrown him. He wished his sister were with him now to guide him; she had such an uncanny ability to calm Abigail. During his walk he'd felt tormented, tormented by her questions and her convincing tone that she really had seen something. He knew his job was to anchor her, but what was he to do? He felt helpless, powerless as her father. He hated this feeling; he was used to feeling in charge in his life.

He was a big fish on the political scene. He had a reputation for solving problems and bringing creative solutions to the table in his job as Deputy Minister of Social Affairs. He needed some comfort from Jackie, but when he put his arm around her she brushed it off. It made him feel more alone in his thoughts. He lay in bed, trying to will his worries out of his head and induce sleep. It wasn't working.

Eventually he got out of bed and headed for the kitchen to warm up some milk. He passed Abigail's bedroom door. He imagined her corn hair spread around her small head on the pillow and felt a strong protective urge to shelter her fragile heart from a cynical world. *She's so pure in her innocence,* he reflected, *sometimes it feels like she's the teacher and I'm the student.* He pondered the idea and then quickly pushed it out of his mind as a silly thought. His job was to anchor her, he reminded himself. This was probably a magical phase she was going through, stimulated by Shona mystical stories from Zukah and triggered by today's stress. *That's probably it,* he summarized. *This is just her usual flightiness gone a bit awry. Her ever-flowing imagination has got her carried away with this smoke idea. Perhaps smoke and death is something Zukah and she discussed; so she imagined seeing smoke.* He took the last sip of warm milk, comforted both by the hot liquid and by the tidy encapsulation of Abigail's behavior. Sleep seduced his mind soon after he put his head back on the pillow; he curled up on the other side of the bed and slept.

In the morning he was able to head out quickly before the family was up. He didn't want to see Abigail for some reason; perhaps it would throw him on this important day. He remembered his theory about her and again it soothed him a bit. He felt overwhelmed by his sister's death as he recalled her limp hand; but knew he couldn't take it in right now. Bill started to reflect on the day ahead. He, his boss, and some other colleagues were meeting with the Prime Minister today and discussing the future plans for the country. Finally, Bill surmised, the Prime Minister was realizing that control was slipping out of his hands and that now was the time to negotiate from a position of strength. At least, that was how Bill interpreted his latest actions. Obviously the Minister was feeling enormous international pressure. Also there was an upcoming meeting at Lancaster House in London to try to negotiate an agreement between all the parties. The Prime Minister wanted a full briefing from many sources, before he headed out of the country for the plenary sessions. Bill looked in his briefcase for his report that he would hand over. It was a comprehensive report, he reflected; he had done a good job, given he only had three weeks to compile it. There were statistics on the casualties of the war. Bill found the figures staggering: Twenty thousand lives had been lost from the start of the war up to now. *What a waste,* he thought.

Bill reflected how overall this was a very tense time in Zimbabwe-Rhodesia. Bill, and his boss Jack, both knew they had to keep their personal views pretty much to themselves. This country was steeped in intolerance; hatred rolled off people's tongues like sour nectar. How on earth would the whites make the transition from a biracial government, under Abel Muzorewa, to a black government with guaranteed white seats? The Muzorewa government had been a massive shift for many of the "when we's" crowd. "When we's" was a great term for them, Bill smiled: those stuck in "when we were in Rhodesia." They were the group in the country who struggled with change; changing their bourgeois lifestyles, Bill concluded, feeling a sneer of disgust form on his face. *Yeah, well, maybe you can't afford that second car next year; too bad. There are some Africans who would like to feed their family and send their kids to school; so you're just going to have to learn to live with less,* he reflected.

He reminded himself again that the white racists were the group he found hardest to tolerate. That group had already overdrawn their meager account at his Love of Humanity Bank of Compassion. Fortunately, he had met some in his racial group he really liked, even though they were racist. He could see they were victims of indoctrination, believing everything they read in the *Herald.* They didn't seem to have the clarity to sort out fact from government propaganda. Those friendships helped him in his dealings with Smith and his party faithful; they had had helped him swallow the response he'd wanted to shout out many a time.

At least the black racists had a genuine cause; it was their country, after all. How on earth did the whiteys possibly think they could generate support for their stance? *They don't seem to get that we're an international disgrace as a country. Over twenty-three years of the world community refusing to trade with us since the Unilateral Declaration of Independence from Smith, then Rhodesia in pariah status since 1976 ...* They obviously believed Smith could pull off his colonial agenda forever; Bill felt the anger rise in him, constricting his heart and throat.

He could see the whites leaving in planeloads. So many had had their heads in an altered reality, ignoring the steamroller of independence from the colonies all around them, that emigration would probably be easier for them than sharing power. *I'd bet my favorite records that today's meeting is going to be tense.*

Later on in the year would be a busy time for Smith as the plenary sessions were scheduled to take place. A new constitution had to be worked out; Bill knew Smith would struggle with releasing white control of the civil service, judiciary, police and armed forces. Couldn't Smith see that the bira-cial government formed recently hadn't from its inception a chance of last-ing? *Margaret Thatcher was a bit of a wake up to Smithy,* Bill sneered, feeling the bitterness rising like bile. He remembered the government meet-ing when Garfield Todd told the gathering that she had changed her position. Mrs. Thatcher, he reported, "no longer saw the Muzorewa-led biracial government declared as an advance towards the restoration of legality, insist-ing now it did not represent a real transfer of power." Bill remembered the look on some of the government officials' faces: They were disgusted that they had been caught with their hands in the till. Boy, it was hard not to be cynical when he saw these opportunists at work, trying to hold onto the reins with their sticky pinkish hands.

So now they were back to the drawing board again. Smith was now consulting the African parties in an effort to get international recognition. *I can't understand how the government thought they could get rid of sanctions without genuine negotiations.*

Bill wondered if he would still have a job under a fully independent black regime. His heart was in the change, and he took solace in the fact that he had a good reputation among the Africans that knew him. The family had close black friends. It wasn't well known among white colleagues; he kept it under wraps, as he might have been further ostracized at work. There were enough snide remarks already, like "Don't get Bill to negotiate for us; he's so soft on the Africans he'll sell us down the river." Others called him a "munt lover"—it riled him, but he pretended to be oblivious. They were aware the Africans found the word offensive, so he knew it was to spite him.

As he thought about the hatred, he could feel disgust take over his mind. He felt a sneer form on his face and congeal with disdain for some whites he worked with. He thought he had left this degree of toxic bile behind when he, with his family in tow, boarded the boat from Northern Ireland to South Africa in 1958. Sure, he knew there would be racism; he was used to relig-ious bigotry between the Catholics and Protestants. But somehow, he didn't imagine the whites being so hate-filled; and mistakenly he had thought inde-pendence wasn't far away. *That was magical thinking on my part, my own flightiness.* Abigail flashed into his mind, but he quickly brushed her image aside. He had liked the idea of working on solutions, of being the jam in the sandwich, the one who was able to bridge racial divides; but it was a lot more entrenched than he had expected.

The whites thought they could hold on indefinitely. Many, reflected Bill, were comfortably oblivious of the racist impact of the charter, particularly the Land Apportionment Act, on the local Africans. In conversation with some of his colleagues he would bring up the details and see their eyes glaze over. *"Did you know that act allocated 50,000 whites 49 million acres of land and a million Africans 29 million acres?"* he would ask. *"They also were given the driest turf in the country; no wonder there are extreme poverty problems in this country,"* his rant would continue. He occasionally heard mumblings of "Oh, there goes that mad Irishman again." At the end of one meeting, an army commander had said to his buddy (just loud enough for Bill to hear), "Pity Boyd won't stuff a gobstopper in his mouth to stop that everflowing political drivel." Bill had left the room pretending he hadn't heard, but it bugged him.

Why couldn't he have any impact on them? He was willing to hear their story even though it bothered him. His father taught him that lesson, and it had been integrated into his very marrow: "Hear your opponent's stories; seek to understand. It's the only way through." His words still echoed, reverberated in Bill's psyche and influenced his daily actions. Powerfully his father had put his beliefs into action by serving both the Catholics and Protestants in his green grocer store in the heart of conflict-ridden Belfast. He didn't seem to be bothered by the criticisms he received and would always say, "If you want to be true to yourself, Bill, you have to let go of popularity. All the great leaders in the world have had to speak their truth in spite of the naysayers around them."

He didn't want to fall into the easy trap of hating the haters. *Hatred is hatred, even it does seem justified,* he would challenge himself. *They're just seduced by royal lifestyles and indoctrination.* He thought of them by satirical nicknames: *Don't expect "Draconian" to budge; he's so tight-arsed he could hold a coin in his sphincter until it rusts.*

He saw the tension in the country building astronomically. Change was sweeping the land like a tornado of uncertainty; political dust was swirling, and each layer of dust muted the senses further. Hearts and souls were being buried under red gauze, muffling the human spirit. The whites walked more stiffly, as if rigor mortis were setting in, ossifying their spirits along with their bones. No one wanted to talk about "the situation." Once the phrase "the situation" came up, there was a flurry of mental activity. People's next words, nimble as acrobats, would divert the conversation to something, anything but reality. Fear built like a subterranean river rising to the surface. Those who weren't completely numb could sense it, cut into it, their foundations mirroring the dry, cracked and exposed land all around them.

In contrast to the anxious word games among the whites, Bill sensed a jubilant mood building in the Africans. It wasn't as if they were celebrating openly, but he could see peace, like a face wash, seep into their expressions.

Their eyes were brighter and smiles seemed to linger longer on their faces. Justice was building in the cumulus clouds up ahead, overarching the land in thick cotton pregnant with rain. They'd been awaiting that cleansing rain ever since a Union Jack was raised on Harare Hill on the September 13, 1890, declaring proudly that a land and culture that had existed for millennia was now firmly under foreign control. Bill shuddered at his heritage. What degree of self-righteousness and brutality would need to permeate a psyche for that act to occur: A flag transported from the soggy emerald-green turf of Ol' Blighty to the land of the baobab tree. The flagpole pushed into the rich red soil, piercing the ground like an arrow, spearing her African heart with a wound that would bleed for nearly a century.

Bill worried about his family, too. He liked the idea of the country reconciling and embracing a long-term political solution, but the impact on his children was uncertain. Stephen and Samantha were older, both being teenagers, so he didn't worry so much about them. However there was Abigail; she was only ten, ten going on five and fifty at the same time. So old and so young, how would she cope with the change? She had black friends like Zukah who would help. Bill had been careful to sensitize his children to racism. He thought he had done a good job. Stephen was the least tolerant, he would say. *Where did he get that?* he wondered. *Certainly not from me or Jackie.* Bill suddenly became aware of worrying about Abigail again. *Put it out of your mind, focus Bill,* he remonstrated with himself, as he drove to the gates of Ian Smith's residence.

His car pulled to a stop behind a gate and a small whitewashed sentry hut. A young man stepped out appearing annoyed at the intrusion. "What is your business?" the white soldier questioned him, lowering his khaki felt hat over his accusatory brown eyes to look more official. His stance bothered Bill, legs wide apart as if to demonstrate his testosterone count.

"I have a meeting with the Honorable Ian Smith today. Here is my ID card." The young soldier snatched it out of his hands and used his thumb to trace his particulars on the card. He glared at the card and then to Bill's face a number of times. *OK, junior,* Bill thought, *lay off the "I have an important sleuth job" routine.* He sat on his hands, trying to contain any reactivity. *We all have enough going on right now, without you having to prove how big your balls are.*

"I'm calling my commander to check the Prime Minister is expecting you," he growled, stiffening his stance and widening his legs another couple of inches.

Bill felt his neck flush with a wave of heat. He felt irritability rise in him like lava desperate to spew. *The country is in a bloody mess, thousands are without land to grow crops and it's my job to find some land. My daughter is stressed; and you think I'm here to waste my time trying to have a meeting when I'm not invited.* He kept it to himself and breathed heavily through clenched teeth. Instead, he asked, "Do you really think that's necessary? My meeting is in ten minutes." His tone was starting to match the cocky young man's belligerence.

"Yah," the guard snapped back and then walked away with his legs as wide apart as if he he had a dozen carrots strung between his thighs, talking to his walkie-talkie, clearly loving his officialdom.

"Damn," Bill muttered, "damn you." *You, young man, are in for a big shock under black rule. You better have your emigration papers ready, because your kind is on the endangered species list.* This kind of male was everywhere in the world, men who pretended their power base was endless; and that herds of skivvies were following them around, willing to obey every order. Bill knew he had a bit of that in him, but on the whole he considered himself a sensitive man. Look at how he raised his children: sure, he was a bit bossy at times but it was for their best interests. He wasn't bossy and authoritarian for the sake of it. Jackie sometimes accused him of being controlling, but he felt it was because he didn't give in to her and the children's every wish; someone had to take the hard line and stand firm. Yes, he was the one that did that for his family; he could stand against the tide even when intense currents suctioned his feet. He noticed Neanderthal man returning, thrusting his hips forward with every step so that his balls bulged in his pants. "You can go," he commanded and left to raise the gate.

That was a close call, Bill thought as he whizzed past the checkpoint. *I could have gotten out of the car and put a whopper on his jaw; that would have woken him up.* Then he remonstrated to himself for dehumanizing a man already dehumanized by an uncontrolled ego. *Have some compassion for a victim of propaganda.* Bill clenched his hand and released it, trying to dispel the disgust he felt so intensely.

Chapter 4

Abigail curled her body into a ball on the one side of her bed, then minutes later threw her body over to the other side. She crunched up tighter, hugging her knees, holding on. Holding onto what, she wondered? *When will I fall asleep?* she kept asking, as if there were someone to answer her. She imagined her mind was now like a record player and there seemed to be only one record available. She felt trapped by it. Aunt Robin's frozen face and limp hair kept flashing at her, a cruel reminder. The memory of the smoke over the dog's head and neck haunted her; especially the way it had followed her hand. After she had been asleep for a while, she woke up startled by an image of smoke coming from Aunt Robin's head. Quickly she put on the light to banish the image. The clock said 3:33 in the morning and she could hear the crickets singing in the distance. She felt her heart beating and her hands were hot. *How will I cope?* she kept asking herself, but no answer would come. After a long time she turned off the light again; but she started to see shadows in her room. Quickly she pulled her duvet over her head. She wished Mom would come and sleep next to her, but how could she ask her? Although her mother had hung in more than usual, Abigail wasn't satisfied that she understood what was happening to her. *I will have to figure things out for myself.* She felt the fear and loneliness in the pit of her stomach, like undigested food just sitting there, weighing down her body and assaulting her mind with countless unanswered questions. Zukah then popped into her head. The thought of his soft face and warm eyes instantly soothed her. *Zukah will understand, I can tell Zukah everything.* Maybe her school friend Madeline too, maybe she would understand. That seemed to soothe her a bit; she felt her head go deeper into the pillow and soon she drifted off again.

Abigail startled at the sound of her alarm. Her head flopped back onto the pillow after she switched it off; and then she remembered why her heart felt leaden. *How will I live without Aunt Robin? I need her, didn't she realize that, why did she have to die? I don't understand how she could just leave me like this.* The questions were a boundless stream, and the morning had just begun. *Who will answer my questions now, who will understand me? I always saved my questions for Aunt Robin when she visited. I'll have to save them for Zukah now.* Dread joined other emotions in her stomach and congealed into a heavy stone.

She remembered her mother had said that she envied Aunt Robin's ability to understand her fully. Abigail knew that her closeness with Aunt Robin also meant a lot to her father. He had told her he admired his older sister. He also said she would have made a gifted mother if she had been able to bear children. This was a gift on both sides, her Dad had said. He told them both that they had wild spirits. He would often say that Robin was the globe seeker and unbridled adventurer of the family. Abigail remembered her father's story about Aunt Robin telling granny that she was going to live in Papua New Guinea. He said granny had shrieked out the country's name, when Robin calmly said she was taking a secretarial job. It was a wild place, her grandfather had said, where cannibalism was still practiced. With all of her strange adventures, Aunt Robin would be able to understand her world. Nothing ever seemed to shock her; yes, if she had Aunt Robin with her she would manage the day somehow. But not now, not now that she had seen Aunt Robin in that horrible wooden box. Her father said she was going to be buried at a cemetery in Canada. He had said to Abigail that they could go and visit together, but that seemed terrible to her. Visit her when she was so deep in the ground, trapped in a box, frozen with a limp hand and hair. If she visited the cemetery, this awful image would never go away. It would get worse, she worried, feeling panicky at the thought.

School was going to be hard today. Abigail felt nauseous; she kept swallowing, hoping it would go away. *I need to talk about Aunt Robin and the smoke over the dog soon; my brain will burst open if I don't.* She shuddered at the thought. *How will I cope at school?* Madeline her girlfriend wouldn't be comfortable; she wasn't good at deep things or at keeping secrets. Abigail recalled the time she'd confided in Madeline that she had a crush on a boy in her class, and Madeline had told the boy her secret. The boy had ignored Abigail for months, then laughed at her once when she'd passed him on her bike in front of all his friends. That memory increased her trapped feeling. She felt her chest tighten.

I have to talk to someone, she remonstrated with herself. *Mom and Dad don't understand, and Samantha and Stephen just laugh at me. I need to talk to Zukah.* She quickly pulled her light blue school dress over her shoulders. *Josef said I couldn't see him until this evening, and that's such a long way away.* What about Josef himself? He would be busy before school; and she remembered he didn't like to be seen with her alone for some reason. It seemed OK if she met him by the river. But if company might be looking he looked scared; his eyes darted around trying to take in the world around them. He lost focus on what she was saying and repeating it got tiring. Really, it was only Zukah that could be fully trusted. She could ask him any question she wanted. He didn't know all of the answers, but at least he thought her questions made sense. Never once did he sneer at her and make her feel small or weird for what she asked. He was a trusted confidant.

School had always been strange for her. She liked geography classes, learning about the wilderness and wild animals all over the world. She often thought about the class on Canada and coastal forests, and what bears like to eat. It was a way of accessing Aunt Robin's world; it helped her to feel closer to Aunt Robin when she wasn't there. She didn't understand why she and Zukah couldn't go to the same school. Her father had said that the government didn't like white and black children learning together, but why not? What was so wrong with that? She already learned from Zukah, so why couldn't she learn from him at school? It was a mystery, as was the fact that all her teachers were white. Some didn't know as much as Josef; that was obvious. She wanted to learn about the land and the plants, the animals and their habits. Sure, her teacher had a passing knowledge of these things, but not as deep as Josef's. Abigail could listen to Josef for hours when she and Zukah were together in his quarters, at the back of the garden. He had stories that had been passed down from his Shona tribe. They were powerful teaching stories about how humans and the land were connected. This was the stuff that excited her. Often her teachers would go on and on about wars in other lands. She had never been to France, and found it hard to imagine a centuries-old scene in a country she had never seen. Her history teacher Mr. Jones could talk endlessly about the French revolution; she saw spittle collect in the corner of his mouth, he was so excited. Abigail didn't get it. This was worthy of more questions: *Why are we studying places we may never see, and from so long ago? Why is war so exciting to some people?*

Abigail had only two real friends at school. One was a boy Ricky, and the other was Madeline. Most of the other kids ignored her. The girls discussed make-up and clothes, but Abigail didn't care what nail polish Greta was wearing or how Jill had gotten a shirt all the way from South Africa. As for the boys, they were reluctant even to be seen talking to a girl, lest they be mocked as sissies.

Madeline wasn't like the girly girls. She always wore jeans and a t-shirt in nature's browns and greens. She loved camouflage clothes, so when she was in nature she would be hidden. Madeline wasn't good at keeping secrets; but she loved to build bridges across the river, or build a frog house and catch tadpoles. Abigail didn't like fondling the frogs, lizards or snakes. She hated the thought of their slimy skin moving over her hand like rough velvet, snakes especially; shivers went down her spine at the mere thought. Madeline didn't mind picking up the non-poisonous snakes, and putting them in a bucket to transport to some other area they deemed suitable. So they made a good team: Abigail did the digging and moving of the big objects; and Madeline did the fondling of the creatures. She was always up for an adventure too. Madeline's sister was really prissy; Abigail was the "sister" with whom she could go a bit wild.

Abigail liked Ricky, too. She couldn't talk to him about personal things, but she appreciated that he had a mind of his own, just like her Dad. He didn't care what others called him; he was popular enough to deal with kid's stuff. Abigail hit it off with him on the school grounds one day. He was looking for someone to kick around the ball. She jumped at the opportunity to show that she could handle the ball smoothly, and hold her own. Ever since then Ricky had seemed impressed with her. They would go for walks in the bush and check out the goggos. Her favorite was the chongololos, long millipedes with burnt orange legs, all the legs moving in unison. One of their games was to see whose chongololo would curl up the fastest, once touched softly with a small stick. Abigail had a good eye for the winners; she trusted her gut and generally won the game hands down.

Zukah, though, was her favorite; he was like an older brother. A brother that she could talk to about anything; even though she only saw him three or four times a year. Each time they reconnected, it felt as if they'd never been apart. Abigail smiled, remembering Zukah telling her she was his "white lily." He had said she was precious to him and that she helped drain from his heart the hatred he felt towards the government, and white people. Her smile broadened as she recalled him saying, "You are like the nectar in the flower, Abigail." When he said the words, she had looked into his brown eyes and she felt her own tears pour down her face. No one else had told her anything so beautiful. How could she ever question whether she could ask him anything? Her true African brother would surely understand completely.

As she was riding her bike to school Abigail thought again about whether she could tell Madeline or Ricky about the death of her aunt Robin and her smoke story. *Definitely not Ricky,* she concluded again; she could chat about creatures and school stuff with him. She wondered if she was going to be able to hear any school lessons at all today. That image in her dreams of Aunt Robin with the smoke coming out of her limp head frightened her, and her heart hurt with missing her. She felt tears on the verge of spilling from her eyes. Any space in her mind seemed gone. What if she asked Madeline to promise to God that she wouldn't tell this time? Maybe if she did promise, maybe then it would be OK.

Abigail looked ahead and saw two Africans walking along the road in the distance. One was older and the other a teenager. Both were moving quickly. One was dressed in white and the other in jeans and a khaki shirt. One seemed to have the same walk as Zukah. Her heart leaped; why would he be going away so early in the morning with Josef? They were carrying bags. She cycled quickly and shouted, "Zukah, Josef, it's me, Abigail." They both turned around, startled. Zukah quickly explained the death of his Uncle Temba and how they were walking to the bus to go to Umtali. They were sorry they couldn't talk; they had to keep walking to the bus stop. Josef was hunched over, and in his eyes Abigail recognized the grief she'd seen in her father's when he'd emerged from Aunt Robin's hospital room. Zukah too looked different; she didn't know what it was, but he was moving all the time he was talking; she had never seen him like that before. She told Zukah about her Aunt Robin; and she had asked when she would see them again, but they didn't know. Josef just shook his head back and forth and Zukah said, "As soon as I can, Abigail. Goodbye, Abigail. Be well, white lily."

Abigail climbed back on her bike when they took the next turn up the hill to the left. Her head spun; her bike was wobbling back and forth on the flat road. How was she to cope now without Josef and Zukah? She didn't even know when she would see them again. She had no one now, no one to help clear her mind. Robin, Zukah and Josef were all gone from her life. She was worried about them, too; she had never seen them look that way. How strange that Zukah had lost his uncle at the same time as she had lost her aunt. Her head felt totally plugged. She would have to tell someone also about her head; if she didn't, she might need a brain operation soon.

She pushed her bike over to the bike rack. Her stomach was aquiver. With Zukah and Josef gone, there seemed no choice now but to tell Madeline. *Surely Madeline wouldn't tell anyone; we've been friends a whole year, and a promise is a promise. I didn't make her promise last time, not to God.* Yes, Abigail concluded as she locked her bike, she could trust Madeline, if she promised God she wouldn't tell.

Abigail slowly moved through the corridors of the red brick building, set in the far corner of an enormous plot of land. Her school had everything: a huge pool, tennis courts, basketball courts, and rugby and soccer fields. Zukah told her his school in the tribal trust lands was a small building, and some classes met under the trees. Class in the open air sounded great to her, except when the thunderstorms came. *What do they do then?* she wondered. *Why didn't I ask Zukah?*

Madeline was sitting in the back of the class and had saved Abigail a seat. She slinked in, pulling her pale blue school uniform down to cover her knees, and pushing her corn-colored hair back over her shoulder. Mr. Jones was about to start and she didn't want to draw attention to herself on a day when tears could spill at any moment, and her heart might get attacked like Aunt Robin's and she would die, a day when her world felt more uncertain than ever. She wanted to be invisible today, invisible until her brain had emptied a lot.

"You are late, Abigail," Mr. Jones blurted. He was British, with a thick English accent, his personality starched as stiff as his ever-neatly pressed shirt. He liked everything to be ordered, desks straight with no crooked passageways; he was constantly pushing desks back in line, as if they were also under his charge and needed controlling. Abigail looked up and felt a hot flush burn on her cheeks. Some kids in the front sniggered, one pointed out her hot streaks of reddened flesh to another. Abigail felt her stomach churn again. She was too afraid to say something. What if some of the dung beetle balls just spilled out; what would others think of her then?

"What have you got to say?" Jones was persistent. He often seemed to spotlight students when they were having a bad day.

"Uh, I got up late, Mr. Jones." Abigail pushed her hair back in an effort to focus.

"Yes, we can see that Abigail. You better make sure you're not late again this week; otherwise you will have to stay behind and write some lines," he huffed, watching the girl squirm under his gaze. She was a bit of a nervous one, he thought to himself. Her head was probably in the clouds; these kids needed discipline. *Probably lacking in their homes,* he reflected; *black help in spades, but no discipline.* Not like his childhood in Sheffield, Northern England. He'd had to get up before the house was heated and make his own bed and breakfast, then ride to school in cold pouring rain. When he was a kid they were made from tough leather, durable and resilient, not like these daisies that pushed over in the slightest wind. How were these ten-year-olds going to cope with the political changes to come? *They'll have to grow up and stop expecting a cotton candy world.* He would help them to mature, to get a bit of character and independence after a life of being waited on like royalty.

Abigail spent the rest of the history lesson overwhelmed by her late arrival, and by all that was happening in her life. With so little space in her mind it was hard to let things go. She couldn't stop thinking about Zukah and Josef leaving; the thought made her brain hurt. Abigail asked God to make sure that Mr. Jones would not pick on her again. She made eye contact, pretending that she was listening. She picked up the odd word here and there: French revolution, bread riots, Marie Antoinette. What it all meant was beyond her comprehension. It was about war, anyway.

We're at war in this country. Why weren't we talking about that? Every night Abigail would watch the news with her family, and before the broadcast there would always be a list of those white soldiers that had died recently. The list was long. Black fighters were called "terrorists," and their deaths were not spoken about. Dad had told her sometime that terrorists were fighting for their country, for majority rule, and that he supported them. He said he didn't like some of their tactics; that he believed in peaceful means to take power. She wondered again why they weren't talking about the war in their own land, about the terrorists, and what was going to happen in the country regarding "the situation." She drifted off in her own world. She had enough to think about right now; revolutions far away were not worthy of her attention, she concluded.

After school Abigail invited Madeline for lunch at her house. She was pleased she had company even though she felt unhinged. Madeline's bike snaked in front of hers, her brown hair flying behind her like a wild mass of thin strings. The only other people on the roads beside the odd car were a couple of African women. One had a huge pile of clothing tied in a white sheet on top of her head, and a baby secured with another sheet on her back. She walked slowly, her head erect, brown eyes fixated ahead. Keeping her eyes focused must help her balance her burdens, Abigail surmised.

On arrival Abigail and Madeline headed straight for the kitchen. Abigail yelled out "Anyone home?" sensing she was the only family member in the house. Abigail started putting jam on Madeline's sandwich, spreading it carefully on the thick brown slab of bread and thinking all the while, *Should I tell her or shouldn't I?* Madeline startled her and said, "That's enough jam, Abigail." Abigail looked at Madeline's warm hazel eyes. Her stomach was quivering, but she ignored it and barreled on. "Something has happened, Madeline. I'll tell you as long as you don't spill to anyone, and I mean *anyone*." Her knife still rested heavily on the bread like an anchor.

"What happened?" Madeline licked her lips, as hungry for the secret as for the sandwich. Secrets gave power; they got people's attention.

Abigail caught the flicker of curiosity in her friend's hazel eyes, the eager flick of her tongue. A funny feeling came over Abigail. She wanted Madeline's support. She withdrew the knife to let her eat at last, but said, "I'm still not sure I should tell you."

"Come on, Abigail, you can tell me." Madeline's feet shuffled as she bit into her sandwich with enthusiasm.

It will help my brain, Abigail reflected. *It's going to help me get it out.* "Promise to God you won't tell anyone. I'll get the bible; place your hand on it and say, 'Promise to God I won't tell anyone.'" Abigail shuffled her feet, desperately trying to read her response clearly.

"I don't need to put my hand on the bible; I can say 'promise to God' right now. C'mon Abigail, you know me." Madeline's eyes moved back and forth like a lizard before it strikes.

"You told Tim I had a crush on him, you told my secret then," Abigail accused, waving her finger in Madeline's face to emphasize her accusation.

"That was ages ago, and I never promised to God; I don't lie to God." She licked her lips emphatically again.

"OK, I'll trust you Madeline, but never do that again."

"I won't. Tell me what's happened."

"Well," Abigail started slowly, her voice quavering with some of the trepidation she felt inside, "my auntie that you never met, the one that visits from Canada for a holiday, her heart was attacked and she died, and we had her funeral yesterday morning. I saw her frozen in a box."

"Why did they freeze her?" Madeline said, stepping back as if disappointed that the topic was not school gossip.

"I mean, not properly frozen, just dead, you know, nothing moved, like she was frozen," Abigail recalled in horror.

"Oh," replied Madeline, shaking her head from side to side as a response, her brow furrowed with confusion.

"It's terrible to lose someone you love," Abigail blurted, a tear running down her left cheek speedily as if it knew this was unsafe company. "Have you ever lost someone, Madeline?"

"No, I only lost a tortoise once, it was eaten by a dog, but my Dad bought me a new one."

"Oh," Abigail replied uncomfortably, not knowing how to continue.

"That's not all you wanted to tell me, is it? Is that why you asked me to swear to God?" Madeline asked her eyes bright with expectation.

"Well, there was one more thing, but I'm not ..." Abigail trailed off, uncertainty building.

"What, Abigail? I've given you my promise," the other girl blurted quickly. Abigail looked at the floor, as if it were shifting beneath her and she wanted to witness it. "What's wrong Abigail, tell me what's wrong?"

"Yesterday ..." she said hesitantly, not sure whether she should go on. "Yesterday ..."

"Yesterday what?" Madeline shouted impatiently.

Abigail started to whisper; something was blocking the sound, muffling it. Something in her felt bad, but she couldn't figure out what it was. A sense of dread cloaked her heart and she felt the pressure. "Well yesterday I was at the river by myself and I saw Bully, you know Bully our bull frog."

"Yah, Bully is often there, I like Bully." Madeline scowled, thinking this was a weird topic for a secret.

"Well after I saw Bully, I ran home. Just as I was about to cross the road a car came down the hill, and a poor white dog got stuck behind the back tire. The little dog died while I was stroking it." A tickle formed at the back of Abigail's throat, and she coughed.

"Oh, that's too bad, Abigail. Is that all you wanted to tell me?" Madeline responded half-heartedly, as if this weren't the kind of secret she had in mind.

"Then ..." Abigail exclaimed, pulling at the waist of her school uniform, her fingers fidgeting nervously while the knife laid dormant in her other hand.

"Then what, Abigail?" Madeline wolfed down another bite, her lips smacking loudly.

Abigail swallowed, feeling she had gone too far to go back. "I saw this smoke following my hand and arm as I was stroking the dog. It was all wispy and was landing on my arm." she swallowed again, staring into Madeline's eyes for a response.

"Was there a fire?" asked Madeline.

"No, you don't get it, there was no fire. This was something spiritual I think, like I was seeing nature's energy or something. I don't know what it was. That's why I'm telling you. What do you think?" Abigail coughed nervously. She felt her body had gone into the deep end of the pool; there was nothing now to anchor her feet; she was completely suspended.

Silence wrapped around them, their friendship was shifting in the void, and neither knew what was happening, just that something was.

Madeline took another step back and took her last bite of the sandwich. She stared at Abigail, who looked a bit limp and weak. "I don't know what you're talking about. Abigail, you're going weird. How could you see nature's energy? You know at church they say heathens talk about things like that. God is looking after us, but only if we're good, my Dad told me; and he warned me never to be around heathens." Madeline stiffened and inched further away from Abigail.

"I'm not a bad person, I'm not doing anything against God. I'm just telling you what I saw." Abigail panicked, now realizing she had made a mistake. She was so desperate for someone to understand; this was going horribly wrong. She should have talked to her mother before discussing things with Madeline.

Both girls shuffled uncomfortably. Neither had the words to explain fully what had happened; only they felt a rift, like a wedge of wood, prying them apart, inserting distance between them.

Madeline looked awkward. "I have to go home and do my homework," she pronounced, not looking at Abigail. She started backing out of the kitchen, as if trying to exit as quickly as she could.

Insecurity rose in Abigail; it moved through her body, collecting at her heart and drowning her voice. "Uh, uh, the bush, what about the bush?" Her tone was high with a desperate tremor.

"I don't feel like it," Madeline said firmly, moving toward the front door. "See you tomorrow," she said, then made a run for the door and ran down the stairs.

Abigail ran after her, the rejection squeezing her chest so she could barely breathe. She knew she was not going to persuade Madeline with her story, but she didn't want to lose her friend. Her mind raced. What could she say so that Madeline would still be her friend? Her voice squeaked, "See you tomorrow," but she knew their friendship would not be the same. She was alone in her world, alone against the world until she could see Zukah again.

Chapter 5

Jackie felt her legs moving painstakingly beneath her. She had drifted through a busy time at the office with intense counseling sessions throughout the day. She needed space to process her day before arriving to the demands of the children and Bill. Abigail had come into her mind several times in the day. Any mental health professional automatically went on high alert when someone spoke of seeing or hearing things that weren't there; it was like a fireman's reaction to an alarm bell. It was to be expected that a mental health counselor would immediately think of schizophrenia or a psychotic episode; either diagnosis made staff shudder. At least a psychotic episode could be brief and the person might recover fully, but schizophrenia, she knew, would be lifelong. Jackie kept getting flashes of the young boy who came into the clinic with his mother last month. She found herself comparing his face with Abigail's. His face had been distraught, as if he had been taken over by bad thoughts. When she tried to get his details he would look through her, and then peer at his mother, unaware that time was drifting by. He was completely lost in his world. What about Abigail—was she lost? Did she leave big gaps in conversation? What about the look in her eyes? Was she hearing voices? The thoughts were an endless stream of disturbing details. *Have I been so caught up with Bill's job, the clinic and the other kids, that I haven't noticed that Abigail was showing signs of mental illness before?* How would that be possible? She spent lots of time with Abigail; how could she have missed this? People don't just become schizophrenic or psychotic out of the blue; she knew that as a mental health worker. There is always a long build-up to these things; and for Abigail to be seeing smoke over a dog there must have been a big build-up.

Guilt gnawed at Jackie all day. It was hard to look colleagues squarely in the eye. Here she was supporting other families; but what about her own family—had she neglected them? Whenever she was stressed her stomach would cramp up; she'd had cramps on and off all day. She was careful what she ate, in case it would exacerbate the acid scouring through her system.

Jackie caught herself going back repeatedly to her training in schizophrenia. Her textbooks in psychology and social work had described a biological hereditary component. There was no mental illness on her side of the family; Bill had said long ago that he had an aunt in England who had been a "little off," but he had never met her. What did he mean by "off," Jackie now wondered, irritated by his comment. Had he been trying to hide something from her, something that would have affected her decision to bear his children? Bill wasn't the secretive type, so why did she think that? Her mind was her enemy right now; she knew that much. Everything else was speculative except her rising stress level. Jackie knew she had to be the strong one right now; Bill couldn't embrace Abigail's struggles, whatever they were. He needed problems with quick solutions, and Abigail's wasn't that kind of a problem. Whatever was wrong with her was woven into her personality, so sensitive and intuitive. Jackie would have to try to persuade Bill to back out and leave it to her; but backing out was not his strong suit. He was a devoted father, but sometimes he was overinvolved. At times she could see that the kids just needed space to figure things out for themselves, but Bill was impatient.

Bill himself was a worry, too, right now. He was in the thick of it politically; he had to walk a fine line between reciting government policy and expressing his own slant on "the situation." She wondered how his meeting had gone with Smith and his cronies. *I hope he didn't step out of line. His "rebel" needs reining in; I keep telling him that. He often just states his mind and then has to deal with major fallout.* She admired that part of him, but it scared her too. He could end up in jail if he criticized the new government. They were not going to take guidance from a "whitey." Sure, he had a good reputation with the Africans; but the new government might react badly if he spoke out against some of their new policies. *This is going to be a dicey time for Bill. This country is going through a political earthquake, and he's in the thick of it.* She could tell he was worried about his job prospects under a black majority government. She didn't think he could bear the thought of being unemployed at home; he needed challenges to stay centered. She didn't think he was emotionally equipped to adapt to early retirement; not in his late forties, that was for sure. *How am I going to cope if Bill loses his job and if Abigail is mentally ill?* The thought was so overwhelming that as soon as it arrived in her mind she tried to forget it, but she felt the reaction in her intestine like a large boulder stuck in her gut.

As she was driving home dusk fell over the land; it was her favorite time of the day. She wound down her window and tried to breathe in the natural world. She was surrounded by bush now; she leaned her head out the car window and listened intently for the crickets. Their back and forth pulse soothed her, seducing her into a moment of "everything will be all right." She had never experienced a natural world that had this impact on her. She could lose herself in it. In Ireland there was little to be heard at night, maybe an odd raven, but it was generally far off. This was one of the reasons they had taken a chance on Rhodesia: They were unashamed nature lovers, and as a family had always been fascinated by African wildlife.

Her car pulled into the driveway. Immediately an apparition of Abigail's stick legs under her school pinafore appeared, quickly opening the gates. She knocked frantically on the car window, gesturing for her to let her in. Jackie's mood shifted instantly; she was hyperalert, back tensing already. She leaned over and swung open the car door.

"What's up, Abigail?" she said, trying to keep calm, but clutching the steering wheel for added strength.

"Mom, I told Madeline about the dog and the wispy smoke, and she ran away. I don't think she's going to be my friend at school anymore. What can I do Mom? I think she thought I was going mad or was supporting the devil." She spewed it out like toxic ooze. "Also, I bumped into Zukah and Josef on the road this morning and they've gone back to their village because Zukah's uncle has died. I didn't have time to talk to him, I so wanted to talk to him." Jackie felt her head whirr like a washing machine's spin cycle. She somehow remembered that she had to be the strong one; she reminded herself to breathe. She looked at her daughter's eyes; Abigail looked tormented, distraught. Jackie shivered and felt her stomach churn. *Anchor, anchor,* was all she could hear in her mind.

"Abigail, I haven't had dinner. I'm tired; let me get some dinner, and then we can chat. I'm sure Madeline is still going to be nice to you." She breathed heavily, her stress rising above her comfort level.

"No, Mom, you don't understand. No one understands me. I hate this world sometimes, I can't deal with it. I really needed to talk to Zukah. You don't understand how important it was to talk to Zukah, and now Madeline won't be my friend." Strands of her hair fell over her face, covering some of the tears that rolled down her cheeks and dropped on her knee.

Jackie stopped the car and reached over and held her. Tears formed in her eyes as unbearable pain like acid scorched her stomach and traveled up to her chest until she could barely breathe. She felt desperate to take Abigail's pain away. How could she protect her? What had she done as a mother to cause this? The guilt swirled in her mind; her world rocked at the sight of her sweet, sensitive daughter's agony. The mother of the young man with schizophrenia, she would have understood Jackie's torment. That was the word: this was living torment. She squeezed Abigail's spindly body in hers, trying to squeeze strength into her bones, into her heart and soul. As she squeezed a feeling came over her that they would get through this. That the journey would be long and arduous, that it would be incredibly lonely, soul-achingly lonely; but somehow the two of them would endure. *Perhaps I'm receiving some help from God right now,* thought Jackie. *Maybe I won't be alone in this. Maybe I'll get spiritual help that I've never had before.* The thought gave her comfort, and she released Abigail and stared into her eyes.

"We're going to get through this sweetie, you and I; it's going to be hard, but we are going to survive this battle." She put her thumb up to Abigail's cheek and her fingers gently wiped the remaining moisture from her daughter's face.

Abigail sensed her mothers' effort to stay with her; she attempted a smile. It felt like it was cracking her face, cracking through the sorrow that had welled around her heart. "Mom, I'm going to see if I can find some chongololos in the garden."

"Yes, do that Abigail; see you soon."

Abigail jumped out of the car. Her pin legs moved quickly in the gold shadow that descended over the garden as dusk shrouded the land. Jackie slumped over the wheel, breathing heavily. Hearing Abigail talk so freely about the smoke frightened her. The hallucination hadn't gone away; her child really must be mentally ill. She felt her heart pounding with the stress. She sensed she would need to hold onto her sanity, much as a rock climber suspended on a craggy rockface holds onto the rope through the steel pin. She had a strong sense that this was going to be the most challenging lap of her life, and its impact would leave an indelible mark on her soul.

Chapter 6

When Bill sat down at the table, he noticed the sheen on it; it could almost be a mirror, he thought. *Maybe it's reflecting our shadows back to us.* He leaned over, trying to see if he could see Smith's shadow reflected. Bill looked around the table at the Prime Minister, Cabinet members, civil service managers; all white men, white men who looked buried by the task in front of them. Some of their drawn faces looked positively ill at the idea of addressing power sharing. He wondered if facial expressions and the racism thermometer could be correlated. These people were in for big-time change, and would fight even microscopic changes. He knew the mentality well; it was evident all over the globe. He called them "the entrenchers." They loved stasis; no matter how unhealthy the situation, they wanted things to remain just as they were. He sensed that their souls were encased in cement. *Just the way they like it,* he thought. *Cement must be one of their most beloved substances, giving an illusion of the external world remaining constant, unchanging, frozen for all time.* The personalities of "the entrenchers" were similar the world over: Domineering, their way or no way, unwilling to integrate another way of being without a struggle. "Compromise" to them meant having to explain one too many times why their position was the correct interpretation, the obvious next step. Bill considered these people's view of the Africans a superb example: They assumed the Africans didn't fully grasp the problem, just because they saw it differently. He found himself listing evidence in his mind as if he were about to defend his theory in public.

So what would they do now that they needed to negotiate more fully with the likes of the Zimbabwe African Peoples Union, and the Zimbabwe African National Union. *Wake-up time,* Bill sneered to himself. *The chickens are all coming home to roost. Time to pull your heads out of the sand.* He looked around the table, expecting to see sand gathered in some ears, or stuck to some foreheads. He scanned the rigid faces, trying to find one with evidence of elasticity. The minister opposite him had laugh-lines around his eyes. *Maybe he gets on well with the Africans, jokes around with them.*

Bill enjoyed the Shona and Matebele sense of humor; it was an effervescent river constantly flowing. *If you like a good josh these are your comrades,* he reminded himself. He would joke around with the Africans at work; their fresh, creative comebacks evened the playing field. It was as if his skin color and theirs had melted in the sun to blend together, painting their bodies in a shared cocoa shade. It was a feeling he liked, and he wished the government understood the rewards of creating a new country that would blend indigenous and Western culture. The experience could be fascinating, transformative, dynamic—a political platform for ingenuity. But the leader had to be powerful, a democrat in his heart, a moderating force, a leader who could meld an understanding between the different groups. Bill had his money on Josiah Tongogara. He liked his overall vision; he had heard an interview in which "Tongo" (his favored nickname) had said that his driving force was his people's need for "land, land, education, land." He had also stated that he favored unity between ZANU and ZAPU. Bill concluded he was an obvious choice, dropped down from heaven on a chute to heal the nation.

This nation sure needs healing, pondered Bill as he saw the men around him start to shuffle papers in preparation for the briefing. He knew Abigail couldn't understand why children grew up with unnatural divisions between races. The others just seemed to get on with their lives, but Abigail with her constant questioning and philosophical spirit was impacted dramatically. It was as if she sensed that the hatred thermometer reading was at the top of the scale. The war was intensifying the resentment; it was a direct mirror of the internal division between the whites and blacks. Bill was determined to keep his son out of the crossfire by sending him out of the country before he got his call-up papers. *No son of mine is going to make this situation worse by killing Africans just for wanting their own land back. I'll do whatever it takes to prevent that.*

He thought of Mr. Testosterone outside. He contemplated whether the guard might have been like his son prior to his army indoctrination. Pumping kids full of war rhetoric, pride and martyrdom because they were "defending their country" was bloody nonsense. *This nation manufactures enough propaganda without my family being subjected to the worst propaganda machine of all, the military. Look what it's done to Irish and British boys back home.* There was no denying that war brought out the worst in the male species; it manufactured and compounded hatred and left the soldiers traumatized, likely for the rest of their lives.

"Right," Ian Smith opened the meeting with a clearing of his throat. "I'm sure you've all heard that Kaunda and Nyerere have both put pressure on the Patriotic Front, represented by Mugabe and Nkomo, to attend the Lancaster talks, and to prepare to make concessions. We all know that the Russians and their allies are still supporting the Patriotic Front. This continues to impact the negotiations; I will go with Sithole, Peter Walls and Muzorewa to the meeting in London. The British are asking for an assurance of white minority representation; this is critical." Smith's lips pushed together in resolve.

Bill started to drift off; he noticed Smith's lips, his fist clenched when he talked of concessions, and his blue eyes narrowing into slits. Bill looked around the table to read others' body language. *They have no idea how much of themselves is revealed,* he smiled internally, sensing he was outside the circle.

Smith continued, "I want to emphasize how important it is for us to hold onto levers of power with the police and judiciary as much as possible." Men nodded around them and Bill also heard a mumble of "hear hear" and "absolutely." "Tongogara is our best choice." Smith went on, clenching his fists again. "I know him personally, as he worked on my parents' farm. They found him to be a loyal servant. He appears open to negotiation and seems committed to accommodating all of the racial groups." Smith pushed his lips together again tightly and waited for questions.

"Honorable Prime Minister, I support Tongogara wholeheartedly," Bill interjected keen to get his voice of tolerance in the forum.

A large man at the end of the table kept shuffling in his seat and kept clearing his throat in anticipation, "Honorable Prime Minister, will our white farmers be protected by the constitution with laws guaranteeing their right to stay on their land?"

"Yes," Smith replied, "I am asking for protection for our farmers. They are critical to the future of this economy." He went on, outlining all of his priorities for the upcoming meeting.

He's sounding a bit more realistic these days. I'm curious what has brought on the change, Bill pondered.

Three hours had gone by and the men were starting to leave. The meeting had been fairly amicable; although the mood was serious, all knew this was a time for the whites to stick together. Differences that would have been highlighted before had been glossed over. No one wanted to stick his neck out; the stress levels were high enough. Nothing had prepared these men for this eventuality. Smith had fed "the entrenchers" with their favorite food, the status quo. His comment a number of years ago was a good example: "I do not believe in black majority rule—not in a thousand years." There had been two solid streams of colonization in this country: colonization of the Africans, and colonization of the psyches of both the elected and electorate.

Thank God real change was in the air; at least he could play a part in recreating the new state under Josiah Tongogara. Yes, that was something to look forward to in his political career. His value of equality for all would guide him beautifully in this next phase of his life. He felt sure that in Northern Ireland he wouldn't have gotten this opportunity to be part of creating a new state. His children could now have the opportunity to complete their schooling with Africans in their classes. It might impede their learning in terms of the British set curriculum for O and A levels, as most of the African children had minimal schooling. As parents, he and Jackie would have to keep vigilant on their children's education.

Bill walked out to his car. He wondered if "Testosterone" would still be there. He felt some compassion for him as he did up his seat belt. This misguided young man could have been Stephen, if he'd gone into the army. That helped Bill as he pulled up to the gate behind the other cars that were departing at the same time. Sure enough, Big Balls was there, looking official, hat even further doffed so only slits of his eyes could now be seen. He kept a salute frozen to his head as if his commander were inspecting him right now. Bill smiled, feeling himself soften inside; he muttered to himself, "Yet another example of the colonization of the colonizers."

He drove home with the radio blasting township jazz. His body rocked to the beat. This was wild Africa, after all, and man, these people knew about making music.

Chapter 7

"Tongogara was killed in a Christmas-Day car accident, only six days after the completion of the Lancaster House talks," announced the dry radio announcer in a thick British accent.

"Mom, Dad," Stephen shouted to his parents in the kitchen, "Tongogara died yesterday; they just announced it on the radio."

"What?" demanded Bill, glaring in disbelief at his son.

Stephen's tone was firm: "I just heard the news. They said Tongo was killed in a car accident yesterday."

"Are you sure, Stephen, are you sure you heard it right?" Bill spluttered, his spittle spraying enthusiastically.

"Yes, of course I'm sure, that's what they just said," Stephen responded defensively, irritated by his father's irascible tone.

Abigail and Samantha, hearing the commotion, gathered on the stone steps above the lounge. "What's happened?" Abigail blurted. "What's wrong?" Her face contorted.

Bill snapped, "Josiah Tongogara has died, who knows what's happened; this is a dark day for this country." He felt his heart sink and deflate. His hopes had been pinned on this man. No one else had such a varied background and was such an obvious mediator between the whites, the Shona and the Matebele. "Mugabe is probably going to get the presidential post, then." Bill looked over to his wife, knowing she understood well the implications for the country, for their children's future, for the future of all Zimbabweans and for his career prospects.

"Did they say it was an accident, Stephen?" Jackie inquired. She put her hand gently on Bill's shoulder, wanting her husband to feel her full support in this bleak moment.

"Yes, that's what they said: they said it was a car accident," Stephen reiterated.

"I don't understand," Bill said emphatically.

"What do you mean Dad?" Samantha inquired.

Jackie looked sternly at Bill, shaking her head as a warning against his response. She had spoken to him many times before regarding his critiques. *If we speak openly about this stuff,* she would remind him incessantly, *we're putting our children at risk.* Stephen saw the grimace and realized his mother was trying to protect his sisters from whatever his father might blurt out.

"Uh, he must have had a faulty car," Bill responded quickly. Flustered he said, "Well, let's just wait until we hear the next newscast in an hour's time—let's just wait until then." Bill quickly walked out of the room and into the garden, wanting to be away from the inquisition so he could collect his thoughts and think through the full implications of this dreadful news for him, his family and the country.

The air was thick with moisture. Bill looked up and saw the dark sky hanging over the garden and the veld beyond, like steely grey gauze blanketing the earth with its ominous presence. The colors in the garden were sharpened with the light. He glanced down at the roses he tended to carefully and stared at their candy pink petals unfurling delicately, their center a perfect cone pointing up to the inky sky. *What's going to happen?* he pondered his mind racing with worry. *This country now has a chance to finally unshackle from its colonial reins and free itself. Thatcher was right on that front; I disagree with her politics but she was correct that the Muzorewa government was not a real transfer of power to a black majority.* Finally this country could be free of the shaming shadow of a pariah state, internationally rejected for its racist policies. This was a grand moment; the Lancaster House agreement meant that Britain and the world would finally accept this country as a full trading partner, with Tongogara as head of state. He had earned a good reputation. Bill had read some British accounts of the talks. Carrington had spoken to a journalist about his respect for Tongogara, and his obvious suitability for leading the country away from its racist history.

Bill thought about his prospects under a government headed by Mugabe. Bill recalled Mugabe's statement to the press when asked about unity with ZAPU, the party headed by Joshua Nkomo, leader of the Matebele in the South: Mugabe had been quoted as saying he would not pursue unity with ZAPU. "It would be sharing the spoils with those who had not shouldered the burden of fighting." If he was divisive toward ZAPU, how would he be toward the whites? Bill walked down the granite driveway, noticing the rockeries with flowers he had tended, the orange and red of the red-hot poker appeared like molten spears in the sharpened light. He walked over the road and moved onto the dusty red path in front of him. He could hear faint drumming, instruments recording the heartbeat of the land. He heard the drums as a lament for the country, a lament for the future, a lament for his family's borrowed time in Africa. So much beauty and pain intermingled on this continent, he reflected. The landscape was breathtaking for him, after the green carpet of Ireland; its wildness burrowed into his soul. Everything had a soulful presence he found hard to describe in letters back home without sounding flighty. He knew he felt it, the common destiny of the people, the pulse of the land, and the formidable spirit of the animals and birds. He had never lived in a place where the morning was welcomed each day by a sky reverberating with twitters and song. The daily infusion of vigor from the natural world emboldened his spirit. What was to happen to this country of great beauty, what political yoke would replace the ever-tightening harness of the colonial reins? Bill turned around, remembering that he wanted to hear the next newscast.

On his return, he found the family huddled over the radio, their voices whispering so that the radio host's voice could be heard. Bill looked down at the family, noting their postures and expressions. Jackie looked worried; he noticed her frown and tight mouth. Such a devoted mother, he reflected, heart and soul with each child, thoroughly embroiled in their lives. Samantha seemed lighthearted by comparison; her tawny hair shrouding her face, but her fiercely determined emerald eyes glowering under the curtain. Stephen seemed a bit gawky in his young manhood. He was like a growing plant that hadn't developed all of its branches so it was a bit off center, his roots still finding their way down to deeper soil. His eyes drank in Abigail's presence, and immediately he felt a pang in his heart. He wanted to stand over her and protect her as a Baobab tree protects a seedling beneath its branches. Her curiosity made her vulnerable, pushed her onto a path where there were few travelers. She was a pioneer, sometimes ill-equipped for the consequences of her adventurous nature. Since she had started talking about the smoke over the dog he had felt even more protective of her. He recalled the recent sleepless nights he'd spent wondering how to spare her the loneliness of being the "different" one, rejected by many who didn't understand her nature.

Just then the news alert recording played and the family was suddenly silent. The voice boomed, "Josiah Tongogara, a much-loved man, a diplomat and appointed President of the new Zimbabwe, has died in a car accident while traveling from Maputo to Chimoio. In another car his fellow traveler Josiah Tungamirai had noticed an army vehicle along the side of the road. He returned to the accident when he realized Tongogara's car was not following behind him. Tongogara died in his arms. Mugabe sends his condolences. Condolences have also been received from many in the British delegation at the Lancaster House talks." When the news went on to other items, Bill asked Stephen to turn off the radio.

"Well, it's true, then." Bill spoke in a matter-of-fact tone, careful to monitor his reaction in front of the children.

"What will happen Dad, what will happen to the country?" Abigail piped in, looking vulnerable and confused, and pressing at her head with her small fingers.

"We don't know, we just don't know. You all don't need to worry; Mom and I will let you know if there's anything to worry about," Bill stated unconvincingly, his shoulders hunching over while his voice trailed off.

"But if we don't have the right leader, the country will suffer," Abigail responded with anxiety in her voice.

She's always one step ahead, thought Bill; it was impossible to shelter this child from the storm. She generally picked up the impending storm before anyone else.

A cacophonous peal of thunder rang through their eardrums. The children rushed to the lounge window, staring at the sky and the rose garden below. A jagged fork of angry lightning slashed threateningly through the darkness..

"Did you see that?" Stephen said to Samantha, pushing her shoulder in the direction of the lightning.

"I saw it," yelped Abigail.

"OK, Abigail, you don't need to yell, my ear hurts," retorted Stephen.

Abigail, sensing her brother's rejection in the dismissal, implored, "Why are you always so mean to me, Stephen?" The feeling of invalidation deflated her.

"Stephen, will you stop criticizing Abigail?" Bill found himself shouting, his voice higher than he intended.

Jackie scowled at Bill and then Stephen, letting out an audible sigh that communicated her frustration.

"I wish Zukah was my brother instead of you," Abigail responded her voice quavering with the hurt. "I wish I could go and see Zukah right now."

"This is what she says! Dad, it's not fair Abigail can say mean things and not get punished. Why do I get picked on?" The boy's face screwed up with tension.

"Both of you," Bill scolded, "stop attacking each other and try to get along. Your sister is younger than you, Stephen; you should know better. I'm going to my room to get some rest; please, everyone, leave me alone." Having taken command of the moment, Bill turned and left.

"Settle down, everyone," Jackie said as he left. "Your Dad is immersed in the politics of this country, and this is upsetting news for him. Just take it easy and let's all get along."

The rain started to pelt the ground and the family moved over to the window for nature's show. The raindrops attacked the ground with such force that red liquid formed angry bubbles, then pools, on the surface of the land. Plants started to droop with the force pounding down on them. Across the road Abigail saw some Africans running for shelter, clothes hugging their hips like thin see-through gauze. *Where are their homes?* she wondered. *Do they have a dry place for shelter?* Abigail caught herself asking questions again. *Stop,* she said inside. *Otherwise your brain will explode.*

She looked above her siblings' heads and saw the smoke circling above them. It was descending over their arms, raining down on their shoulders, landing on their clothing. She liked looking at it. It was alive; it swayed here and there, formed different patterns: sometimes a zigzag, other times circles. *It's like it has its own personality,* she thought secretly. The smoke she'd first seen over the dog was now everywhere; it must have followed her home that day. It seemed comfortable with her, comfortable because she could see it and felt no need to chase it away.

Abigail reflected on how much her life had changed in the time since she'd first seen the smoke (*almost a year now*, she realized), and since Zukah and Josef had departed. When Mr. Smithers told her Josef wasn't returning, because he was now the village headman, Abigail remembered crying for days. Nothing could take the loneliness away. She felt her heart was going to crack open and dry out like a dead cricket in the sun. She was scared; and no one seemed to understand what she was afraid of. She felt different from her siblings; their lives seemed so normal compared to hers. She was the sensitive one, the family philosopher, and the one that everyone worried about. She hated that; she hated Madeline for pushing her away and telling some of her classmates. Since then people had looked at her strangely, as if carrots were growing out of her ears. When she went to bed at night, the feeling of her heart cracking and drying up always came up. She hugged her stuffed dog Bruno tighter, hoping he would protect her heart from getting attacked and shattering with loneliness.

Abigail felt the only person who was trying to understand her was her mother. She worried about her mother worrying about her. When she'd told her mother that the smoke had followed her home and that she could see it everywhere in the sunlight, her mother looked sick with worry. Abigail saw the frown on her forehead intensify, and her eyes looked frightened. That frightened Abigail; she needed her mother to be on her side. Why couldn't her mother understand her fully? Why couldn't her mother act like Aunt Robin? She would have understood the smoke and been curious with her. Her mother, though, did seem to understand how hard it was to hear the other kids snickering as she walked by, especially when one said to her, "Madeline thinks you're crazy because you see things that aren't there." She hated that girl; she hated school since Madeline had rejected her and told others about the smoke story. Her Mom had helped her, helped her to see that the girl was a weak person if she had to be mean to her. That made Abigail feel a bit better in the moment; but all the time the loneliness and confusion was there. She felt her brain was getting weaker; the loneliness was now taking over her head along with the confusion. She worried about the dung beetle balls building, whether she would able to pass exams with the dung beetle balls in her brain. She worried whether she would have a friend again that she could trust fully like Zukah, or an adult that she could lean on like Robin. She still had Ricky to play with, but most of the girls were ignoring her these days. She had been talking to another lonely girl, Gillian, but she didn't feel she had much in common with her except that they were both lonely. Gillian didn't like the bush, nor was she adventurous, so Abigail felt no desire to spend time with her other than in class. She also worried about her family. Things were changing, and she could feel the growing uncertainty in people around her, but no one said anything. This was one thing she could never understand: why people felt things and pretended they didn't, while everyone else around them pretended, too.

At least I can talk to my mother about these things, but sometimes I wonder if she thinks I'm a mental case. She had found a paper in her mother's bag one day and it said something about signs and symptoms of schizo-something. Abigail was only able to read a bit before she heard her mother come down the passage, but she noticed that her mother had underlined several lines. One line she remembered was "seeing or hearing things." She had asked her mother one day what schizo-something was and her mother started to cough suddenly, and went to the kitchen to have a drink and ignored the question. It was at times like this that Abigail felt she had no one fully on her side, no one who understood how she felt and what she thought. There was no one around that didn't judge her in some way, like saying she was a heathen or had a brain problem. On those days Abigail remembered hugging Bruno so tightly in the night that he left a dent on her skin, where she had pressed him into her. It was then she would wonder why Aunt Robin died, or why she did not live in the same city when she was alive so she could have seen her more; so she would have less dung beetle balls. She also questioned why she didn't have Zukah for a brother. It wasn't that she didn't love her family; it was just that she wanted to be understood fully, for people to see what she saw in the world, for answers to the endless questions she had. Sometimes she yearned for a family that could help her remove the dung beetle balls one by one, so she could think normally again and maybe have more friends.

The rain was now over and everyone had left the lounge and had gone outside. She heard her mother shout her name: "Abigail, come outside. What are you doing in there?"

"I'm coming Mom," she said, pleased that someone had missed her.

"What were you doing, Abigail?" Jackie asked, looking suspiciously at her daughter for any more signs of a mental illness.

"Nothing, Mom. Why are you looking at me strangely?" Abigail felt the loneliness harden again around her heart.

"I'm not looking at you strangely," Jackie replied. "I was just wondering what you were doing, that's all."

She felt a stab of guilt at the realization that her daughter had read her thoughts. Guilt was a common feeling for Jackie these days. She wondered what she had done as a mother to cause Abigail to have these strange experiences. She had not seen the mental illness coming on, she had never contemplated schizophrenia as a part of any of her children's lives. The doctor wanted her to persuade Abigail to come in for an evaluation as he felt she likely needed medication. When she had asked her if she wanted something to take the smoke away she had said no, that she had started to like the smoke. Jackie felt guilty at the thought that the girl wasn't getting the right care, and feared her condition would deteriorate.

Yet besides the smoke conversations all her other thoughts seemed fine. She was able to follow conversations and not drift off as if hearing things, so Jackie felt reassured that she was not having auditory hallucinations. In fact, at times she appeared the strongest in the family, which Jackie found odd. How could she have a mental illness and be the family anchor? Her set of symptoms was certainly unusual; and in none of the mental health literature did Jackie hear of anyone seeing smoke. Hallucinations from her experience were tormenting for the client, often adding to the individual's self-loathing. Abigail was different; she found the smoke comforting. The psychiatrist she had consulted with was old school, and his analysis was black and white. The points he raised didn't really fit Abigail. Jackie wanted to protect her from the likes of him. Schizophrenia was about losing touch with reality, but Abigail's constant questioning showed that in a way, she was more willing to face reality than anyone else in the family. Jackie was left uncertain, confused, guilty, overwhelmed, and most often helpless.

Jackie assessed Abigail's facial expressions one more time. She looked confused and a bit lonely, but not tormented. *Maybe she's just really sensitive. She definitely sees right through people's masks, she knows when people are hiding from the truth.* Jackie sighed. *Maybe she doesn't have schizophrenia after all; maybe it's something that isn't as serious.* She would stay vigilant, as she knew some illnesses could come on suddenly. Jackie had discussed the medication issue with Bill, and she let him know that the smoke was still there. Bill had been adamant: No daughter of his was going to take medication for a misdiagnosed mental illness. He thought the idea was outrageous. The girl's imagination had just gone a bit wild; the smoke would just go away, one day, he said. Sure, he was worried about her being different at school because of her philosophical bent, worried that other children seemed to find it threatening. He had asked the Smithers whether Josef was ever coming back, because he hoped she would see Zukah in the future. Both he and Jackie agreed that Zukah seemed to settle her. When he was around, her spirits went up, and she seemed so much more alive. When they received the news that Josef wasn't returning, they asked some local Africans whether anyone belonged to Josef's village. They wanted to find out if Zukah was looking for work; they thought he might be interested in coming to work at the farm up the road. No one they had asked so far knew of Josef's village in Umtali.

Maybe Bill was right after all about Abigail's wild imagination, Jackie reflected, bending down to pick up some of the rose petals that had been released by the rains. She rubbed at the soft velvety smoothness. Perhaps she needed to relax more; maybe the family needed a holiday. That would help, she thought, making a note to bring it up next time Bill appeared relaxed. *We are just going through a lot of stress as a family. Maybe this will all go away once the country settles as a new nation, and has a stable government.* She clenched her fists, desperately wanting to affirm such hopes.

Chapter 8

Bill heard a knock at his office door. "Come in," he shouted, trying to tidy up his desk at the same time.

Jack peered over his half-lens tortoise shell glasses, his hazel brown eyes glaring straight at Bill. "Did you read today's press releases yet, Bill?"

"Not yet. Why what's up? Take a seat." Bill shuffled nervously.

Jack slumped in the wooden chair in front of Bill's desk, clutching a paper in his hand. *He looks older these days,* Bill thought. *His face is redder, too. I wonder if he's drinking more to deal with the stress. He's been a great boss, always fair and a decent man to the core; but he's not good at managing change; that's his weak spot.* Jack's body had stiffened like an ironing board, as if it had forgotten how to bend. His tousled brown hair was like a weaverbird's nest with twigs in all directions.

"Bill, everyone knew Tongogara was a strong man and would stand up for democracy. It's awful; this should be a moment of immense glory for this country, finally freeing itself from the horrors of colonialism. Now someone is responsible for sowing dark seeds in this land. The loss of Tongo is devastating; I've felt sick ever since I heard the news on Boxing Day. My gut says we're in for trouble." Jack's voice rose as his fist pounded a stack of papers; he had never been good at coping with frustration.

"Shush, keep your voice down, Jack. There are going to be spies out catching those whites who don't embrace the changeover," Bill responded, anxiously trying to guide his boss out of danger as he pushed the papers back together frantically.

"Look, Bill, if I can't say what I mean anymore, what use am I in my position as Director of Social Affairs." Jack sounded irritated. He stood up and started to pace the room like a crazed cat trapped in a cage, occasionally glancing at Bill over his glasses.

"Jack, we want to do what we can to help with the transition. This is going to be the toughest change we've had so far, and it just got a whole bunch tougher with Tongo gone. I want to do my part to help this country. So many have suffered under the old regime. It's hard for me, too, Jack. You know me, I am not the walking on ostrich eggs type, but this is a really delicate time, especially for us whiteys." Bill stood up and leaned against the window, his frame resting at an angle "You don't need me, Jack, to point that out: For the people who have suffered, for my family, I want to do all that I can to make this bad situation turn around."

"Well, I'll think about it, Bill, but at this point I feel like giving up. Anyway, there should be a government memo in your internal post. It's addressing the land issue. There are stats such as 4,500 white farmers are on 75% of prime land compared to millions of African peasants trying to exist on land as bone-dry as the flipping Karoo." Jack started to pace again, his pace quickening the longer he spoke. "Of course the land needs to be redistributed; you don't have to be a bloody commie to get that."

"Yah I'm with you Jack," Bill mumbled, his fingers twitching.

"But it needs to be done fairly or the country will lose its economic backbone." Jack raised his voice again and glared at Bill.

"Sshh Jack, we don't want the whole department to hear, do we?" Bill queried irascibly. Jack carried on a little softer but his scorn suggested resentment at having to adjust his tone. "We need the white farmers to hang in and provide food for the next several years until the Africans are in a good position to replace them. Land distribution can't be done quickly; if it is it will move this country onto a precipice in no time."

Bill, sensing Jack was on his political pulpit and just needed to spew, leaned back in his chair, breathing consciously to keep calm as Jack continued, "Hopefully race relations will be such that progressive white farmers will stay. So much depends on Mugabe. Who knows what Mugabe will do about the land issue? He wants to be seen to redressing past wrongs, but the way he goes about it will be critical to this country's stability." Jack collapsed onto the chair again, unaware that he had just gone on a rant.

"By the way," he added, "this news just came in: this department will be spearheading a major refugee repatriation program as soon as the election is over." Jack put down his glasses and stared over at Bill, not removing his gaze for some time. "It's going to be an astronomical undertaking; thousands of refugees in Mozambique and Zambia are desperate to return home." Jack returned his glasses to his face and started to purse his lips, a signal of building tension that Bill knew well. "We'll need to coordinate with UNHCR. It's massive. Read up about it and then let's meet; you and I are going to move right into the government spotlight with this program. Our ministry is going to be under heavy political pressure to get this right. Lots of lives are at risk and we can't have a single soul dying in the camps because of lack of food. Otherwise, we'll be strung out for the hyenas." Jack leaped out of his seat and moved toward the door, his body looking crumpled under his equally crumpled suit. "Hang in there, man. We have a rocky road ahead, you and I. I'll pop in later and talk about the returning refugee program."

"See you later Jack," Bill responded, relieved his boss was leaving him to his own thoughts for a while.

Bill held his head in his hands, massaging his scalp, trying to alleviate the tension he felt building. Jack might hang himself politically; a pretty big rebel lurked under his disheveled suit, and he sometimes got careless. Bill knew from past experience that he, too, had an inner rebel who could take over when pushed too hard. Jack had gotten away with it under the Muzorewa government; he had been tolerated. However, Bill remembered Jack sending him in when the political heat was intense. *It's different now; the whites have lost a lot of power, so we have to be seen following the party line. If Jack's drinking gets bad again, he's not going to be able to handle the pressure. It'll be hard enough for me to keep muzzled; I'm not exactly the muzzle-wearing type.*

Bill moved his fingers to his neck, kneading the tension. He felt on edge, as if he had one precipice in front of him, one behind him, and one on either side. He knew he was on his own; he couldn't count on Jack for support; and Jackie at home was too preoccupied with Abigail's mental health to be there for him. Jackie was pretty labile he concluded, one minute she was thinking Abigail's ideas were just a sign of intense stress, the next minute she was convinced she had schizophrenia, and was browbeating him into forcing her to take Modicate, a medication for schizophrenia. He still felt really bad when he remembered the day he raised his voice to Jackie about not having his daughter treated for schizophrenia and Abigail walked in. He couldn't look her in the eye at the time; but he remembered the sound of her voice, like the strangled whisper of a songbird with a noose tightening around its throat, and the dejected slump of her body like a willow burdened under its own branches. "Am I going crazy?" she'd squeaked. "Mom and Dad, is that what you think?" He hadn't known how to respond, and Jackie had been so overwhelmed in the moment that she had cried. Eventually Abigail had left, but the moment still haunted him. His relationship with Abigail hadn't been the same since. He still didn't know what to say to her.

He looked through the papers on his desk and found the internal post pile. He found one labeled "Returning Refugees" and started to read, pushing his fingers through his hair and kneading his scalp. After some time, Bill looked at his watch: three-thirty. Just then there was a rude knock on the door.

"Come in," he growled. "Oh, hi Jack, howzit going?" Bill mumbled, knowing he was likely to witness another tirade.

"Well, what did you glean from the report, Bill?" his form looked more crumpled than earlier.

"Yah, OK man, I've got some figures on the number of displaced persons and demobilized troops; it's about six hundred and sixty thousand, estimated. They're mainly in Mozambique and Zambia, but there are also thousands in various countries in Eastern Europe that will return."

"Six hundred and sixty thousand and more, you're pulling my leg." Jack laughed, rocking up and down in his wheeled chair.

"No, I wish I were. They want a big number to move to a township outside Salisbury, so that should be easier for us in terms of arranging for food and supplies. But apparently there are going to be camps all over this country. They want these soldiers to turn into the new farmers," Bill added in a tone that was trying hard to mask his anxiety.

"That's impossible—these guys have been fighting a war, they aren't just going to roll over and get excited over a packet of seeds. Who in the hell is making these decisions?" Jack's voice cracked angrily, and Bill noticed that his boss' hand had an ever-so-slight tremor. *He better not be drinking on the job*, Bill thought, terrified by the tremor. *If my boss loses it, I'm going to be kicked out too, no doubt about that. How in the hell will our family survive on Jackie's wages?* Bill started to pull at the skin around his fingernails.

"I spoke to the Ministry of Manpower and Development earlier, Bill. They're talking to ZANU-PF about a directive on minimum and maximum wage levels when they get into power. I can understand them needing to bring parity to the working poor, absolutely, but what in hell are they doing penalizing top earners so soon. It doesn't make sense; these people will just leave and go to South Africa, and gut the government's economy at the same time. Can't they see if you turn it into a socialist state overnight there's going to be no foreign investment? We need foreign investment badly if we're going to provide schooling and health care for seven million Africans now." Jack flipped over papers in his hand impatiently. "Oh, I have a news clip to give you, the political pulse of the day." Bill instinctively started to breathe again. There was no way he wanted an argument with Jack, not when he was this volatile.

"Here it is." Jack lowered his voice and read the clip, the cynicism evident in his sarcastic tone, then sighed, "We need a pragmatist and a moderate; now that Tongo is gone, we're left with these Castro wannabes."

"Hang on, Jack. Your pessimism is colonizing your mind. We haven't had the election yet; sure, Mugabe and his cohorts look like a shoe-in, but who knows? Something else may happen, and Muzorewa may increase his support. Let's just hang in there and bide our time, not make so many quick judgments. It'll help us get the job done, and put some jam on our bread at the same time. You're on your own, but remember I have a voracious brood back home, and we sure as hell can't live on Jackie's wages."

"Well, well, the cool voice in a cauldron of political turmoil," spat Jack sarcastically. "Keep holding on, Bill. Someone has to anchor us to earth in this tornado of uncertainty."

"You know I keep a cool head when things are intense. Why not take a back seat, and let me take charge of Operation Returning Refugees, when the directive comes. Hang in there, Jack; I'll spearhead this operation."

"Yah, that might be a good idea, Bill."

"OK, Jack, I'll take it on, and you chill. I'll report back to you regularly. We'll know where we stand in a week. If there are any developments in the meantime from the ZANU-PF crowd, I'll let you know." Bill felt the tension building between his shoulder blades.

"Yah, keep me posted; just in case I get a call from the Ministry I want to be up to speed. This country is in total chaos right now, Bill. You can't have an unelected government in charge since mid-December and not expect earthquakes every day," Jack ranted. "Sure, the Brits have sent some troops; but they have no idea what it's like to be in on the day-to-day operations. No one knows what's going on, or what's going to happen after the elections; and there's so much speculation that everyone seems unhinged. ZANU-PF is already trying to give directives, like it's a *fait accompli*. Thank God it's only a week before Election Day; February 27, 1980 will be the day this country economically plunges into the crevasse. Oh well, I should look on the bright side, shouldn't I, Bill?" Jack waved his hands in the air as if conducting an orchestra. Bill breathed; instinctively he knew to keep a low profile when Jack was this intense. "At least we'll have some direction, although I'm not sure I'm going to like the policies of these full-on commies." His fist thumped Bill's desk at the word "commies."

He's for an African government, but unlike me, he's a fiscal conservative, mused Bill. *He's going to have a tough time; I'll need to be vigilant about him losing it.* Bill looked up and smiled at Jack in a desperate effort to placate him. "No problem. I'll let you know of any developments straight away."

"Thanks Bill. Hey, take it easy and say hi to Jackie and the kids." Jack looked up and smiled, his hazel hawk eyes scrunching up with warmth as he got up to leave.

"Will do, you too." Bill opened the door quickly. He exhaled with relief once his boss left. *Thank God we got through that one.*

On the drive home, Bill purposely took the long route. He had so much on his mind that it felt like his brain was going to start leaking out his ears, it was so full. Jack had really let him down; clearly he wasn't capable of holding his ground in a climate of mass uncertainty. Bill realized he not only had to pull off his own job in an intensely chaotic political atmosphere, but he also needed to keep his eyes on Jack and try to muzzle him as much as possible. If Jack was going to try to drink his way through this they were in for trouble. Bill knew Jack's impulsivity increased dramatically when he went on his drinking bouts.

Home life was tough, too, he pondered, feeling stress building in his neck. Abigail was distant from everyone these days, and Jackie wasn't able to relax as she used to. He often caught her staring at Abigail as if the girl were a science experiment whose results Jackie had to track. *Why can't she leave the girl alone? Abigail has enough to deal with,* he reflected, irritated by Jackie's anxiety. Jackie was a devoted mother, but she seemed to lose her ground when the kids were going through a lot. *She takes it on emotionally; it must be the job, seeing all those distressed clients every day makes her think the worst with her own family and friends.* Bill started to feel irritated by her job, but then realized his also brought a great deal of stress onto the family. *She can't help taking on Abigail's worries and catastrophizing. Thank God Samantha and Stephen are doing OK, both doing well in school, thank goodness.* Bill's mind started whirring, trying to remember Stephen's age; thank God he was too young for the army and the war was over. What a relief Jackie didn't have to face her son going into the bush, killing Africans fighting for a return of their homeland. That, if added to Abigail's problems, would have pushed her right over the edge.

The sun had started to descend. He marveled for a while at the scorched red and orange light filling the sky like a painter mimicking fire. The bush reverberated stillness. It seemed pregnant with the anticipation of the night cloak that was soon to cover the land. He passed several acacia trees standing erect on the landscape, proud and bold with their skin of protective thorns. The land had remained untamed, with its belly exposed in a primordial state. Thank God the family had moved here; there was a magnetic pull on this continent unlike any other he had experienced. This place was alive with sadness and joy strung together in a poignant blend. *This is where the world's heart beats,* he mused, *along with the African drum.*

Chapter 9

"Hey, everyone, I'm home," Bill yelled, swinging open the kitchen door enthusiastically.

Jackie stood at the stove, stirring vigorously at some substance in a small pot. She looked over angrily. "You're late and you didn't call."

"Hey, hold your horses! I'm just in the door; can't you greet me first?"

"What do you want Bill, the red carpet rolled out as soon as we take in your presence?" she replied in a biting caustic tone.

"What's up with you, Jackie? I've had a hard day at the office; I was looking forward to spending a quiet pleasant evening with the family. Where are the kids?" He tried to sit on his rising anger. He felt his fingers twitching, and the back of his neck start to heat up with tension.

"They're in their bedrooms doing their homework; someone has got to keep the home fires burning. Must be nice to come home to all the tasks being done," she added, her voice escalating.

"You're gunning for a fight. Back off Jackie, or I'll get angry too."

"Are you threatening me, is that what you're doing?" she shrilled.

Bill stormed out, throwing down his briefcase with a loud thud; then slammed the door and strode furiously down the passage. *This is the last thing I need,* he mumbled to himself. *The country is falling apart, my boss is unhinged and so is my family.*

Just then Abigail opened her door. "What's wrong, Dad?" she said looking scared. "Why did you slam the door?" Her green eyes brimmed with fear, and her shoulders cowered like a hyena's.

"Abigail, just stay out of this," he yelled, feeling the blow to her heart as soon as he said it. He saw her body crumple and her spirit wilt under the force of rebuke, before he raced to the master bedroom and slammed the door behind him.

Abigail furtively opened the kitchen door. She saw her mother in a heap on the dining room floor, hugging her knees, her body rocking in grief. Abigail felt her heart split open with the pain of it all. "Mom, why are you on the floor, what's wrong?" she said plaintively, trying to contain her own tears that felt as if they were about to burst from her.

"Abigail, I'm sorry, you don't need to worry. Your father and I need to sort something out, that's all." Mom said, scrambling from the floor.

"It's not me, is it Mom, it's not because I told you that I'm hearing someone else's thoughts in my head is it, I didn't upset you, did I Mom?" she pleaded, tears rolling spontaneously.

"No, Abigail," Mom coughed.

"Why are you coughing? Mom? You always do that when you're trying to hide something from me." Abigail's eyes searched imploringly for reassurance that she was not to blame.

"Abigail, I'm just going to go outside for a walk—please let me be. I'll be fine in a while."

Samantha opened the door. "Where's dinner, Mom? What was that noise?"

"Your Dad has had a tough day, that's all—I'm going for a short walk, maybe you and Abigail can set the table."

"OK, Mom." Samantha turned to her sister. "What's wrong with you, Abigail. You haven't been crying again, have you?"

"Nothing's wrong with me—mind your own business," Abigail scoffed back, sensing the family couldn't deal with another fight. "Let's set the table, Samantha, and help Mom." Abigail wiped at her cheeks to erase evidence of her meltdown.

"I don't feel like setting the table. I'm hungry," Samantha replied, opening up the fridge to look for a morsel she could devour.

Abigail felt angry with her sister, but she knew if she challenged her a fight would break out; she was too concerned about her parents to take a chance. *Samantha is so into herself,* she thought, *always in her own world, just like Stephen. I seem to be the only one trying to keep the family together.* Her shoulders tensed with the weight of distress. Abigail wondered if she should go outside and talk to her Mom, or try again with her Dad. *Best set the table first,* she thought. *Mom will be cross if I haven't done it, and Dad scares me right now.*

Slowly she opened the drawers and found the placemats depicting African wildlife. She wished she could escape right now to the game park. When she was there, nothing else mattered. She remembered watching the glide of the giraffes as they moved across the land, long necks pointing up to the tree line, mottled bodies blending into Africa's earthy tones. Her favorite creatures were the elephants. She loved watching them as they moved away. Their behinds always looked a bit comical to her, big chunky bottoms with sagging skin and a small tail that swung back and forth with a spirited swish. None of the animals frightened her except for the hyenas. Their eyes shifted in their faces, and their jaws often opened in strange, toothy grins that dripped saliva. Abigail always felt they looked as if they had been caught in an evil act, as if they were trying to slink away from the evidence of mauling some innocent creature. They were the only animals she really resented getting prey; the rest she was able to tolerate. She had heard their sick, haunted cackle late into the night; just the thought of it still gave her the shivers.

"Have you set the table, girls?" Jackie walked in, breathing loudly as if she was trying to calm herself down as quickly as possible. "Where's Samantha, Abigail, didn't she help you?" She sounded annoyed.

"It's OK, Mom. How are you feeling?" Abigail spoke softly, trying to soothe her mother with her calm tone. She sensed that she had rocked her mother's world, and that Mom's fear had risen with news of her hearing voices.

Mom visibly softened. She stretched out her hands as if to lift a burden from Abigail. "You don't need to worry, Abigail; I'm fine. Now go and tell everyone that dinner's ready. I'm serving it up now."

Abigail quickly moved down the passage, poking her head into her brother and sister's room to announce dinner was ready. Next she furtively knocked on her parents' bedroom door. "Dad, Mom says dinner is ready," she called out, trying to make her voice sound calm so he would be reassured that the storm had passed.

"OK, Abigail, I'm coming." Bill slowly heaved his body off the bed, rubbing his eyes as if he could wipe out his memory of the day: Jackie's anger, Jack's instability and his own remorse for snapping at Abigail.

The family members all sat in their familiar chairs. Abigail leaned forward, delivering each person a plate filled with roast chicken, peas and carrots. Tension sat between Bill and Jackie like a thick brick wall. Bill was silent; he looked askance at his wife, distrusting her ability to manage her mood. *She's no idea what I'm going through,* he thought internally; *lucky she's not the Deputy Director of Social Affairs of this country.* His job sizzled on a political hot plate set at a fierce heat. Clearly Jackie could not be counted on to support him these days. *I haven't been able to lean on her since Abigail first talked about the smoke. She ratchets things up unnecessarily. I told her it was just Abigail's imagination; but obviously working in the mental health field makes her so flipping suspicious. This is the first time a family member's sanity has been questioned and she has just flipped out.* He looked over at her, feeling the distance between them. *She's changing into someone I don't know; how can that happen after we've been together for nineteen years?* His analysis left him perplexed. His mind kept whirring; never before had both the country and the family been facing so much change. One tidal wave had followed another; no area in their world seemed stable. *Be patient,* he said to himself. *The old Jackie will come back.* She had become coated with sharp quills of late, but he willed her prickles to soften.

Stephen, seemingly unaware of the goings on, talked about his rugby match against an opposing school team. "You should have seen them, Dad. They were flying up the wing and I just ran as fast as I could and grabbed his legs and I pulled him down, he was just a couple of meters from the goal line—man, it was great!"

"Good for you, Stephen," Bill mumbled, trying to generate some enthusiasm for the boy's accomplishment.

Abigail stared back and forth at her parents as if she were watching a game of tennis; each time one made a movement she noted it. She could sense the anger in both of them. Her mother's lips were tight. She looked very serious, as if she were sitting on top of fireworks that were about to explode. Abigail's father, meanwhile, avoided eye contact with her mother, and his brows were knitted together into one long line across his face. Abigail wondered what she could say that could bring some laughter to the table.

"I spoke to the new gardener next door, Philemon," she offered. "He told me Mr. Smithers was putting the chemicals in the pool the other night, and he fell in and he was in his suit." Abigail laughed, joined by Samantha and Stephen.

"Serves him right," Stephen retorted. "He was mean to Josef—not letting him come back and get his stuff because he had to leave the job."

Abigail watched closely for her parents' reaction, but neither said anything. It was as if her mother weren't with them at the table, as if she had gone somewhere else. Her Dad looked too on edge to say anything; she didn't remember things being this bad between them. It was making Abigail nervous.

"Hey, Dad, can we go walking in the bush on the weekend?"

"We'll see Abigail," he replied tentatively, but his eyes remained on Abigail's mother.

Abigail watched the smoke dance between them, as if trying to help them break down their anger. Abigail talked to the smoke in her mind: *Please, smoke, try to help them love each other,* she implored.

A thought popped into her mind, as if someone had inserted it between the dung beetle balls. "I think we need a holiday. Why don't we go to Victoria Falls? We all enjoy ourselves there, and I would love to see all the animals and birds again. Please, Mom and Dad, can we go to Victoria Falls soon?"

Bill and Jackie looked at each other, both taken aback at the idea, neither knowing quite what to say. "What do you think Mom and Dad, can we go?" she repeated lightheartedly.

Jackie looked up, coming back to the family from wherever she was. "Well, Bill, what do you think?" she said quietly.

Bill felt relieved. It was as if somebody had waved a wand and magically healed the family. He couldn't put his finger on it; Abigail really was remarkable at times. Lately this enhanced ability to know what to say when silence and tension immobilized others' tongues, had become even more apparent. She would make a great politician, he thought.

"Uh, well, if you think it's a good idea Jackie, I'm game. The rains are drying up, and we always have a good holiday there. It will be after the voting for the new government. It's probably a good time; it will take a while before the new government is inaugurated. Then my job is going to be crazy with finding accommodation and food for the returning soldiers and refugees."

"Yea!!!! Does that mean we're going, can we go soon, Mom?" Abigail blurted, feeling elated. She could barely contain herself on the dining room chair, she was so relieved that her idea had worked.

"Great, Mom and Dad, I love Vic Falls! Can we visit the crocodile farm when we're there?" Samantha interjected excitedly.

"Yeah, those crocs are quite something, especially picking up the baby crocs, too," Stephen commented calmly.

"Well," responded Jackie, "I need to take some holidays before year end in April, so that would work for me at work. But are you sure, Bill? What about the resettlement programs? Can you take a week's break?" Jackie leaned over to make eye contact with Bill.

Talk about schizophrenic, he thought. *One minute she's snapping my head off like a piranha and now she's cooing like a pigeon.* He straightened in his chair; he knew he needed to handle this one carefully to move out of the storm. "Well, big numbers haven't started arriving yet; it will take some time before the entire six hundred and sixty thousand displaced persons return to the country. The new government will need to be inaugurated before we can start moving on any initiatives. I'll clear it with Jack, but it should be OK; it's only a week."

"So we're going Dad? Sounds like it's for sure," piped in Samantha, taking another helping of chicken at the same time.

"Dad has to check at work," Stephen muttered.

After dinner Jackie and Bill cleared the table. Bill checked that the children had all gone to their rooms and closed the kitchen door.

"What's up Jackie? There must be something bugging you."

"Sorry, Bill, I'm sorry, that was uncalled for. It's Abigail. I'm really worried about her. She told me this afternoon that she not only sees the smoke, but she says she's hearing a voice in her head every now and then that tells her what to say. She described it like someone has put a thought in an injection and inserts it into her brain."

"Are you sure this isn't just her imagination running wild again, Jackie? You know how she is; she does lift off at times." He kept his voice soothing, desperately hoping not to retrigger the piranha.

"No Bill, we need to face it, she's mentally ill. You know and I know that these are signs and symptoms of schizophrenia. Now she's seeing and hearing things that aren't based in reality."

"Look, Jackie, I know you're in the field, and it makes it worse. But you heard how clever she was tonight; she always seems to know what to say at any given moment. She's with us, not floating off somewhere else. I don't buy it, Jackie; I know she says she sees smoke. I think her imagination is going a bit wild, that's all. Look, I'm not willing to consider medication, if that's what you're about to propose. I won't go there, Jackie, not when I'm not convinced there's anything wrong. I won't have any child of mine taking toxic pharmaceuticals for no good reason. We both know the side effects are really serious; they would turn her into a zombie overnight, given her sensitivity. Just try to relax a bit more, the holiday will do you good. C'mon, let's go for a walk and relax; we've both had a hard day." He moved to put his arm around her, but felt her pull away suddenly; he winced, thinking the vicious fish had returned for another round of biting.

"Bill, I don't want to get angry again, but you don't get it, our daughter is ill and she needs medication so she doesn't get any worse. Please, Bill, can't you see it? I don't want to give her medication any more than you do but it's necessary. We have to face reality." Jackie paced the kitchen floor, unable to make eye contact. She felt sick at what she was saying, desperate for some relief that her precious daughter was going to be OK.

Bill breathed, *I have enough on my plate, and Jackie hasn't a clue what's happening with me at work. Why can't Jackie just relax and see what happens? Why does she ratchet up so easily?* His understanding of schizophrenia was that it affected the sufferer's ability to take part in everyday conversations because their heads were so full of other thoughts and images. *Abigail is with us; she isn't floating off somewhere else. Sure, her imagination is rich; but she stays with the conversation,* he reiterated in his mind, feeling outraged at the thought of his daughter being labeled schizophrenic. He was also now questioning his wife's ability to maintain her equilibrium. He concluded quickly the discussion was circular; there was no way of penetrating Jackie's mind. She was immovable. How could he respond in a way to delay action? In the meantime he would pay closer attention.

"Look, Jackie, I hear your concern. Let's give it another couple of months. This may be her imagination filling in for the loss of Zukah and Robin. Let's go on a vacation and all relax together; in the meantime I'll observe more closely. Right now I'm not worried about schizophrenia, but I'll see if I pick up anything worrying between now and the end of March. Can we delay making a decision, Jackie, please?" He looked at her imploringly, willing peace in his mind, peace for the family, his wife, the country, peace for all.

Jackie shook her head, trying to shake the worry out, trying to make space for a different outcome for her daughter, but the worry seemed to fill all the space so other thoughts weren't able to take hold. She didn't have the strength to argue, and she knew Bill was having a tough time at work. What would be the point in insisting on medication now if it were going to cause intense family battles? That would worry Abigail more, and maybe her symptoms would worsen. She picked up family distress like a shark smelling blood in the ocean. Delaying it made sense for Bill and her, and maybe for Abigail too. She just prayed the symptoms were not going to get worse in the meantime.

"OK, Bill, I'll wait until after our vacation; but please monitor carefully in the meantime. Please, we don't want her to get worse and for this illness to erode her mind. I know this is really early onset; normally it happens in the late teenage years. You never know with mental illness; it sneaks up on people. One day they seem fine, and the next they're floridly psychotic, oh God, it's too awful to think about." Jackie started to cry, softly at first, but when Bill went over to hold her she collapsed in his arms, her body rocking with searing pain that was rising and flowing out of her. "How could this happen to our precious Abigail, Bill, how could this happen?"

Bill held her closer, trying to squeeze the pain and worry out of her. His heart felt like it was sagging with the sadness all around him. He wanted to reassure her, but he knew she wasn't ready to accept any reassurance. He started to worry himself; maybe Jackie was right and Abigail was good at masking normalcy. *And how reactive is Jackie going to get? Will the piranha take over my sweet loving Jackie?* He started to feel nauseous at the thought of both of them ill. *No, I can't think about that right now, not while the country is in a crisis with Mugabe likely going to the helm. There's so much change right now. I need to stay focused, focused on what needs my attention right now.* He felt tightness in his chest. Worry began to invade his mind, displacing the feeling that everything would work out all right eventually

"We'll just hang in there, babe," he told his wife. "Let's just hang in and see what happens. I'm sure it will all work out." His voice trailed off. He had wanted to sound more comforting, like a man with faith, but his tone conveyed the vulnerability he felt. Uncertainty was shaking their world; he sensed the foundation cracking. Small cracks at first, but that was how crevices, gorges and deep canyons were carved out of the earth, he thought, one earth-shattering moment after another. He pulled Jackie a bit closer, pulled her into those weak places in his body, trying to smother them so all would be well.

Chapter 10

Zukah listened intently while Josef talked with the elders in the village. They sat under the Jacaranda tree, nestling in the shade that was rare in the African veld. Few trees could create enough of a shadow on the ground to provide relief from the midday sun. At this time of day the sun had fierce power, crinkling leaves, burning up drops of water like a thirsty god sucking up any moisture from the earth. The summer god, thought Zukah, was always parched, drinking all the moisture on the earth's surface, leaving the ancient land scarred with red marks of age.

Four men, including Josef, sat on the ground in a circle. The older men carried long sticks, not only to help them walk but to symbolize their age and status in their rudzwi. Zukah looked at their faces. His father appeared the youngest; his skin was relatively smooth on his cheeks compared to the other men whose faces were lined with experience. Zukah looked at the lines that had created furrows in their flesh. He imagined that each line reflected hard-earned wisdom, collected in the soul as a treasure trove for all to draw on. *Did that mean Zukah himself had gathered little wisdom?* he pondered, feeling his skin, smooth and rubbery under his thumb.

The dunhu headman spoke first, addressing the Nechombo, who was the medium for Mhondoro, the tribal spirit of the village. His blood red eyes looked at the tribal chieftain and lastly Josef, the new village headman. "You have returned, Josef; the spirits have spoken," he said in a low growl barely audible to the group.

"We have returned from the diviner," Josef reported to the Nechombo, dunhu headman and tribal chief, his head nodding in deference to the men. "Aaay," he said "there is a snake in the village and he is a danger to our community. This dark one released the cobra near Temba, so he was killed while he was working in the fields. The diviner said it is our task as a village to find the snake, and Temba, as a Mudzimu, will help us. By doing this we will help heal the people of their troubles."

Zukah knew that when there was a suspicious death in the village a diviner who lived far away, a stranger to the group, needed to be consulted about the circumstances of the death.

"Aaay, aaay we lost Temba to a snake," the dunhu headman nodded to the tribal chief. His red eyes drank in the news to a different depth; his soul seemed transparent in the red pools. Zukah felt transfixed by his eyes. Their depth seemed endless, and it appeared as if he were drawing on centuries of experience for this moment.

"We will need a medium for Temba to return," the dunhu headman continued. "The caterpillar has left the grave. He is a wandering spirit now, but we will call him back in time to inhabit one of us. Temba and Zukah have a strong spirit connection; Zukah then will be a good medium for Temba to inhabit."

The tribal chieftain placed his sinewy black hand on his stick, and banged it on the red earth in approval. He nodded, and paused. The group waited for the Nechombo's response, the vessel for the Mhondoro. They watched his face while a force took over his mind and body. His eyes glazed, his hands started to shake as he left his present world and gave himself over to spirit. The men stared at the earth, in honor of the Mhondoro's presence in the group. Zukah sensed the world around him; stillness and spirit hung in the air like suspended raindrops. He felt the Mhondoro's spirit in the Nechombo, the energy diffused in the group. Zukah felt it like strong energy swirling around his body. He now felt held, propped up, supported. He had admiration for the Nechombo as a vessel for such a big spirit. He knew from the stories of his father and the elders that the Mhondoro protected the tribe. His father had also told him that the Mhondoros were similar to the tribe; they also had a hierarchy of power and influence. The least powerful was the family Mudzimu; then the lesser Mhondoro and then a Mhondoro of greater stature. The most powerful Mhondoro, his father had said, was the great spirit of Chaminuka. Zukah had learned that Chaminuka was the master, that he surpassed all the other Mhondoros in the spirit world in his abilities. It had sounded to Zukah at the time as if the Chaminuka spirit must be God, however his father had corrected him and said God's name was Mwari, and unlike Chaminuka, Mwari had never been a man. It was the role of the Mudzimu and the Mhondoro to protect the tribe, and to manipulate nature or events if necessary for the good of the tribe. "Never anger a Mhondoro," his father had warned. "They can hold the rain, or send locusts to eat the crops if they are enraged. He is there for us, but if we betray him he can punish us."

The group continued to wait patiently for the Nechombo's response. The chieftain's large brown eyes looked over the group, and then glanced at Zukah intently. His face was small, and his cheekbones still visible under the wrinkled jet-black skin. Zukah felt a shiver go down his back, like a spirit already in his body. Tensing, he focused on holding his body still. He realized fully the seriousness of the discussion, and felt humbled by his name being spoken in the presence of these wise men.

The Nechombo started to blink rapidly; it appeared to Zukah that he was coming back into this world. The Nechombo breathed and spoke slowly, each word melting in the heat as soon as he had spoken it: "Zukah has a big spirit, and his love for Temba is strong. Zukah is a good vessel for Temba to return." The Nechombo took another deep breath, shutting his eyes, and then continued in a raspy voice, "The Mhondoro knows who the snake is. He also knew Temba would die from the snakebite, but did not interfere as Temba's ordained path is to be a spirit guide for the village. He will hold that truth about the snake in our village. It will be healing for Temba to help locate the snake through Zukah's help." He slowly placed his stick back on the ground; indicating a decision had been made with the Mhondoro's guidance.

"Aaay, my son Zukah," Josef said nodding looking at his son with pride. "He will carry Temba's spirit and help us find the snake."

Zukah watched the men carefully. His father had prepared him for the meeting. He had spoken to him about the honor of carrying Temba's spirit and told him that he was a likely vessel. His father had also explained the rituals involved in becoming a medium. He had said that Temba, in caterpillar form, would be called back to the family in a Kurova guva ceremony. Zukah sensed that Temba's spirit visited him at times. He felt comforted by the idea of Temba being with him all the time; he would still have his uncle by his side after all.

Zukah had also felt the unease back in the village since Temba's death. The community was less sure of itself; something had shifted and the bonds were not as solid. Temba's death had left a shadow; even when the sun had departed the land, the shadow still lurked. It sat between the village members. It was there in the fields when they were growing the mealies, plowing the land, tending their crops. It followed them to the river to get water; the women carried the buckets on their heads but they looked around them more, as if a wild animal were slinking in the undergrowth about to attack at any moment. It slithered in between the group in the evening when they sat around the fire, and listened to the elders tell the stories from many ancestors ago. Even the dogs moved with dis-ease, grabbing at food more voraciously; growling as they devoured each morsel as if it were their last. Children played; but every now and then they would stop, as if something reminded them that their fun could end at any moment, that life was more serious now, and that everyone needed to be more vigilant. Zukah hoped the village would restore and heal with Temba as a Mudzimu. The village hopefully could return to peace; his father had assured him that it was possible, if they managed to detect the snake.

The Nechombo spoke again, the words slowly oozing out of his mouth, addressing the tribal chieftain: "We will need to sacrifice a bull to calm the spirit of Temba; also beer must be brewed and drunk tonight to appease his spirit from the wrong that was done to him. The village will honor Temba tonight." He banged his stick twice on the ground, indicating that the guidance from the Mhondoro was now over. Cracks shattered beneath his stick, dusting its tip with a caress of rust-red soil, dry and powdery.

"Aaay," nodded the tribal chieftain, "a bull will be slaughtered. We will drink beer and Josef will speak to Temba tonight to accept our offerings."

"Aaay, I will speak to Temba and ask him to accept our sacrifice," replied Josef, aware of his role in the rituals.

The four men stood up slowly. Josef waited for the men to gather their aging bodies together; and when they were ready he respectfully followed behind them. These were the men who had the responsibility of guiding the rudzwi. Josef took great comfort in their wisdom. As a newly appointed village headman he now had more contact with them, but he remained aware at all times that he was a sapling sprouting in the shadow of an ancient tree. His thoughts were young, ill-formed, limited in awareness and knowledge. These were his teachers, and he in turn could teach his children about the wisdom of the elders. He wondered why the white bosses he worked for did not seem to draw on the wisdom of their elders; his boss' parents seemed without a role in his eyes. Just because their bodies were feeble, were they assumed to be useless? It confused him; he had been taught that drawing on the elders was like drawing on the deepest water in the well. The water at the bottom of the well had the closest contact with the bowels of the earth; therefore its properties were of a substance that the surface water could not understand. He remembered meeting Mr. Smithers' father who would occasionally visit the family for lunch. He had seen him as an elder, with his white hair sitting straight up on his scalp, as if he had had a fright one day, his pale blue eyes deep-seated in his face, the lines of loneliness around his mouth. When Josef worked in the garden, he overheard the family talking while having lunch outside. He had been shocked to hear the family talking about Mr. Smithers' father as if he weren't there, as if he were invisible. It troubled him; how could they know which path to take if the young saplings were making the decisions without the elders' input?

Josef felt pleased to be back with his people. *I have my status restored now. I am no longer a servant, endlessly pleasing people who don't understand me, who take advantage of me because of my skin color. With the guidance of the elders, I can heal my heart from the bitterness I collected in the white world.* Josef felt relieved to be around guidance again. Without the elders guiding the village, his community would break down. There would be more hatred between people, the man who put the snake in Temba's path would not be found and so there would be no opportunity for reconciliation.

He had his own hatred toward this man who had orchestrated his brother's death, but he knew the elders would help him heal that, too. The frozen part of his body would come back to life again. He would be able to embrace this man in time through the rituals and healing offered to him; and hopefully they would live in peace in the same village.

Josef looked ahead of the three men and saw the village alive with activity. There were children playing with a goat, trying to get him over a fence to feed on other grasses. He could hear their faint laughter murmuring across the land. He saw women in movement. One was pounding corn in a wooden container, her body gyrating powerfully under the fierce heat. As he moved closer he saw women carrying water on their heads in clay pots, moving toward the cooking area. Their slim bodies were erect, clothed in swirling cloth that hugged their bodies as they moved slowly, barefoot on the red soil. Each day in the village was a new day; the village had countless activities to perform in order to secure its survival. He no longer worked set hours as he had worked for Mr. Smithers; here, where there was light there was work to do. As soon as the sun ascended the activity in the village started to hum around him. He felt the sun offering her energy to help the villagers perform the tasks necessary for survival. The women mostly collected firewood and water from the nearby river. They cooked at night and pounded the corn. Many men were in the fields planting crops and plowing the fields with cattle. He remembered tending the cattle for many years, taking them each day to an area where they could forage. For the rudzwi the cattle were precious; they gave milk and meat when needed. He worried about the cattle in this dry weather. If the land did not receive rain they would have to be killed. He knew for the rudzwi without rain they would fall on hard times, and many would know a hungry belly.

Zukah felt energized seeing the village preparing for the ceremony for Temba. He felt his uncle's spirit visit him momentarily, nudging at his heart, letting him know that he was there. Zukah followed some men with pangas into the bush. He wondered how they would choose the bull to be slaughtered. He listened as they spoke about the age of the bulls and which one was the best animal for the ceremony. He watched as all their panga's together hit the neck of the bull, saw its blood flowing, the animal's heavy frame collapsing in the grass, its feet still kicking angrily as the life slowly oozed out of its body. He saw the red earth initially drinking the blood like rainwater and then rejecting it as it sat on the soil forming a murky pool, staining the grasses. He watched closely as they skinned the body with their knives. The animal looked strange to him, coated in a red flesh; its skin collecting all around; in a lifeless, snakelike coil as it baked in the sun. Then Zukah and other young men were called to transport parts of the bull to the cooking area. Zukah held onto a leg, feeling the warmth of the flesh like soft rubber under his hand. He felt the blood dripping through his fingers like oozing tree sap.

He watched it smudging the earth, as if alerting the whole village of its
sacrifice for Temba.

A fire was now licking the late afternoon air in the middle of the court-
yard area. Sticks had been collected and an older man was feeding the fire's
appetite slowly, knowing not to give in to its greed too soon. Temba had
taught Zukah about building and sustaining a fire: He called the fire the
"greedy one," the one that likes to devour everything quickly. "Never give in
to the fire. Take charge, Zukah, and then the fire will give you the warmth
and heat that you need." The boy's heart sank a little as he remembered
Temba's voice and the kind way that he had instructed him. Zukah felt
pleased his father was back in the village, but he still missed Temba. His
uncle had given him so much of his attention, watching him carefully like a
growing plant, making sure he was growing at all times in the right direction.
Zukah felt some of his roots had resurfaced since Temba's death. As if they
were confused with their direction now, they needed guidance before they
could dig deeper into the soil again. Zukah hoped when he was a vessel for
Temba's spirit his roots would confidently drive to deeper ground, anchoring
him during this tumultuous time.

The sun was only somewhat visible now at the edge of the horizon. Its
dying fiery tendrils lit up the landscape in a last warm glow before it kissed
the day goodbye, and gave over to the moon. Zukah saw the villagers gather
around the fire, and the smell of cooking flesh overwhelmed his senses; it
had been a long time since he had eaten meat. Beer was collected in large
calabashes, and sat in the middle awaiting the right moment for consumption.
As night slowly fell on the land more villagers started to gather around the
fire. They sat on the ground, waiting in silence for the ceremony to begin.
Zukah noticed that the children behind their parents seemed a little restless.
One played with a dog; the chickens were moving in and out of the circle,
unaware of the danger of the fire. Zukah heard the crickets begin their evening song. It lulled his senses; he remembered Temba telling him, *"The
crickets like to sing to our souls. They remind us the bush is always alive with
danger. Listen to their song, Zukah; it will soothe you when you heart is
troubled."* Zukah watched the sparks fly from the fire, like spirits intent on
joining the villagers' evening rites.

Zukah's father stood and the villagers gave him their full attention. Josef
picked up a large calabash and placed it in the container holding the beer. He
held the calabash above his head and shouted, "Temba, we have brewed this
beer and killed a beast in your honor. Please accept our offering. We ask the
snake: Kill no more. You have taken our beloved Temba; let the village
know peace again." Zukah saw his father place the calabash near his mouth
and drink a small sip. He invited the village to join him. With reverence that
had no need to hurry, they passed the calabash around, all partaking in the
brew. There was a ringing silence in the air as if all were willing Temba's

spirit to join them. Zukah looked at all the bodies suspiciously, wondering who among them could have placed the cobra in the field to attack Temba. He stared intensely at the faces, trying to intuit who might be responsible by noting which eyes seemed dark to him, which person was drinking the beer in celebration. It sent a shiver down his back. Why would they kill his uncle, a man who had been good to all? The confusion nestled into his mind, unsettled him down to his restless roots. Life was not the same without Temba.

After the elders had eaten, Zukah took a portion of the meat. His mouth watered before he placed any in his mouth. He wanted to savor it the same way that he was savoring his memories with his uncle. Slowly he bit into it, tasting the charcoal along with the flesh. He remembered the bull's angry feet and its fighting spirit. Maybe the bull would give him strength, strength to find Temba's killer, and strength to move on without him in human form. He looked around and hoped the same for the village; strength to move on from the loss of his lion-spirited uncle who had given so much to his people.

Chapter 11

"There it is," shrieked Abigail, rocking back and forth on the seat next to Samantha and behind her parents.

"*Mosi oa tunya.*" Bill turned around, staring between the seats at his daughters' wild-eyed faces.

"What does that mean again, Dad?" blurted Abigail.

"'The smoke that thunders,' that's what it means. Look at the mist rising like smoke above the land. The Zulu-Ndebele call it 'water rising as smoke' but I prefer the Kololo saying because the smoke does make a thundering sound."

"Who are the Kololo, Dad?" Samantha inquired, fully alert now that the Falls were in full view below.

"They were a tribe on the run from the Zulus. They lived on the Zambian side of the falls." Bill peered over Jackie's shoulder at the same time to stare at the sight below. The land was a khaki color dotted with green sponges for trees. He saw the chasm in the land; it looked as if a Godlike force had forced the land apart to reveal the raging beauty below. He saw the mist rise over the escarpment, its moist fingers reaching up to the sky as if wanting contact with the heavens. His heart felt bathed in beauty. He leaned over and squeezed Jackie's leg, sensing the tension in her body in spite of the wondrous site below. Her eyes crinkled warmly at him. Her breath fogged on the glass of the airplane's tiny window. Bill felt his whole body sigh. He sighed that his family were on holiday in one of the most wondrous parts of the world, sighed that he had survived work and all its drama. He was relieved that the country had survived the election; Mugabe was now in power. At least they had some stability now. He sighed that this country of great beauty, and immense pain, was making some progress in healing the long-festering

87

wounds that had deprived them all of peace. *I have a lot to be grateful for,* he reminded himself.

"Aah, we've arrived at last," he muttered barely audibly, but loud enough for those around him to sense his relief. He prayed internally that the family was going to be able to put their worries behind them and relish a full immersion into this spiritually renewing world. *What would it take for Jackie to relax?* he wondered. Through the corner of his eye he noted her hunched shoulders, the permanently worried look on her face and her distance from the family. *It's as if she's gone into survival mode,* he pondered, *as if her pain were too great to be shared.* He wondered if some of her own family history had bubbled up and accentuated her reaction to Abigail. Maybe Abigail's talk of smoke had re-triggered the feelings of helplessness Jackie had felt as she'd watched her father die of stomach cancer. Her trauma had been obvious the few times she'd been willing even to discuss her father's death. Bill had tried to soothe her but nothing had seemed to work, as if the experience had left a permanent tear in her heart so deep that nothing would heal it. He leaned over and squeezed her knee again, trying to bring her back to the present, but he could see his efforts were fruitless. He imagined her heart shrinking ever smaller, surrounded by a wall that seemed to be thickening against her conscious will. They hadn't talked about Abigail's mental state since the day the family planned the trip. He had kept up his side of the bargain and observed her more. He felt guilty as he realized that Jackie had been the one to deal with Abigail's preoccupations in the last couple of months, while he had been consumed with his job and all the political changes since the election.

He thought back to his conversations with Abigail since he had been assessing her more closely. She seemed to have her feet on the ground, he thought; she was able to discuss her homework and what happened at school. However, he noticed that much of her joy seemed to have drained from her, and she looked more fearful. Normally Abigail would have opened up fully to him; they had always had an effortlessly strong bond. She was less accessible now, especially since she overheard Jackie and him questioning whether she was mentally ill. She had retreated since then into a lonely void somewhere; her trust in the world around her had been undermined. He had asked her a number of times about the smoke and the voices; she had muttered an evasive response as if she didn't want to talk about it. Bill sensed she was trying to protect the family; she was so sensitive to others' needs. She likely concluded that telling her mother about the voices had tipped her over the edge. *That child is always right on; she reads the family like a book.*

As the plane began its descent, Bill wondered whether Jackie was right. Was the girl ill and now afraid to talk about the matter? *No, not Abigail.* His heart burned with the thought, and he felt his shoulders tense up at the idea. How could she be so intuitive with others if an illness was taking over her mind? She was not herself, though; something had happened since the smoke conversations. Initially she seemed to like it, as if it comforted her. *What on earth could it be then?* he asked himself, feeling desperate to get an answer, desperate to reassure Jackie and Abigail. He didn't have Jackie's mental health knowledge; but based on his own intuition he didn't feel Abigail was either psychotic or delusional. She looked lonely, misunderstood and confused. He had noticed lately her new habit of rubbing her temples and massaging them. She looked confused when she did it. It saddened him to see her sweet face and big eyes all crumpled, confused and sad-looking; it broke his heart just to think about it. He could feel the pain rising, but he pushed it down by holding his breath. This pain felt too deep to acknowledge, lest it tear him apart. He didn't want to lose his innocent family philosopher to some god-awful illness. *Please, God, save my Abigail from some ravaging illness; it would be too much to bear.*

When he heard the plane's landing gear squeak on the runway, he looked around him and closely observed Abigail and Samantha's faces. Samantha looked overjoyed, her eyes flickering with energy under her heavy fringe, while Abigail's excitement seemed muted; normally she would be bubbling over in anticipation of a nature holiday. She gave him a smile and he returned it; but he saw fear sitting in her eyes. It hurt to acknowledge it, so he quickly looked away, but the shadow of the hurt lingered. He felt a blanket go over his heart and smother some of his feelings.

When the family arrived at the colonial hotel, they started to gather the bags the taxi driver had deposited in a heap. Just then Abigail whined loudly, "Do I have to share a room with Samantha?"

"You girls always share a room on holidays. What's wrong, Abigail?" Jackie's tone was anguished, and she looked to Bill for reinforcement.

"Yes, Abigail and Samantha, we only booked three rooms because you always share," Bill reiterated gently. He put down the two suitcases in his hands on the tarmac, but still held the handles as if to convey his impatience for a lengthy discussion.

"I don't want to share a room," Abigail retorted, her voice rising higher and sounding desperate.

"Abigail," Jackie scoffed, her face contorting, "keep your voice down. It's too late to change it." She quickly took a scan of the area around them. A group of elderly tourists were walking towards the hotel. She hoped they had not overheard the family argument.

"I can't share a room, you don't understand." Abigail's voice cracked with emotion.

"Abigail, keep your voice down," Jackie repeated, annoyed. "What don't we understand?"

Abigail pulled her body away abruptly. "No one understands me, no one, I have no one." Tears started to roll down her face. Her eyes were smothered in liquid. Samantha and Stephen walked away, whispering to themselves.

Jackie's tone revealed controlled anger. "Abigail, what is it, for goodness sake. Why don't you want to share a room?" Jackie braced herself; she felt her body stiffen as fear and anxiety burbled in her stomach. At least this time Bill was here; she was tired of carrying this family burden on her own, watching her daughter descend into a pit of darkness with more and more bizarre accounts of her reality.

Even when Abigail said nothing, it was enough to look at her face and see the hollowness and fear in her eyes. Jackie's thoughts kept flashing back to the young boy who came in with his mother all disheveled, the illness holding him in a vice grip. The look in Abigail's eyes haunted her, followed her to work, sat in the middle of her chats with friends, stifled her vocal chords and kept her from voicing what was really troubling her. She had always taken pride in the way she had embraced pain, acknowledged it, dealt with it and moved on. She'd always told clients, "Face the pain as it comes in a small wave initially; if you run from it, it will catch up to you eventually and build like a tsunami on a wild ocean."

This time was different, though. She didn't have the words to describe the soul-harrowing nature of it. She had been thinking and dreaming about her father lately, too, lying there in a hospital bed, his pain so unbearable he couldn't speak to her, but communicating the excruciating torment with his eyes. She shuddered, recalling the dream in which she was with her father at the hospital: His lips had looked parched, and she knew he was desperate for a drink, as if his life depended on it, but she had her hands tied behind her back.

Her concern for Abigail carried an added burden of shame. She wanted to protect Abigail from others' judgments; she knew from her job how harsh some people were to the mentally ill. The illness triggered such fear in them that kind, well-intentioned people were suddenly capable of saying cruel and vicious things. What could she say to her friends? "Oh, by the way, my daughter sees wispy smoke and hears a voice in her head; apart from that everything is great"?

Jackie knew the situation had pounded a wedge ever-deeper between her and Bill. She wanted to feel close to him, but right now she had to keep her guard up. Too much closeness felt threatening; sharing the pain might crack open her heart. She tried to compartmentalize the pain, contain it in an internal vat, and pretend it wasn't there, but the feeling that she was going to crack at any time didn't go away. As she waited for Abigail's answer, Jackie felt on the edge of a cliff, the soil beneath her crumbling, her toes digging in with all their might for a hold.

Abigail looked down, her shoulders hunched, and for a while there was silence. Eventually she looked up furtively through her web of hair; she clenched her hands, desperate to melt the ice that had formed over her heart, desperate for someone to take away the loneliness and confusion. She pushed at her temples, trying to make space in between the dung beetle balls for her thoughts to come through. *What can I say that will make my parents understand?* "At night I need to talk to the spirit," she tried to explain. "That's our time to talk; Samantha would think I was weird talking to a spirit." She felt relieved to get the words out, but fearful of her family's reaction.

Jackie looked over to Bill, her eyes searching for his reaction. How were they to handle this one? It felt beyond her ability; she might fall over the cliff if she took it in fully. She felt herself retreat; go somewhere else, anywhere but here where she had to accept fully that her daughter had given over to madness.

Bill lowered his voice, placed his hand on Abigail's shoulder, and in a protective and tender tone said, "Abigail, I know you imagine that you hear a voice, we all hear our heads say things, but they're not spirits; it's our own mind talking back to us."

Abigail looked at her mother's face and hesitated to continue, but it was too late to stop now; her mind had cleared enough space between dung beetle balls for her thoughts to form quickly. "The spirit tells me things now every day and every night. It drops thoughts in my head. It even tells me what's going to happen in the future; it sends me signs, like certain birds mean certain things. It hasn't told me who it is or why the smoke from the dog follows me around, but maybe it will tell me soon, and I can let you know." Abigail looked at her parents' faces. Her mother looked far away. Her glassy eyes scared Abigail; she needed her mother to hold her hand and protect her, but the woman didn't even seem to hear her. Abigail searched her father's face for acceptance. She saw compassion and tenderness in his eyes, but she saw fear too. Her heart ached as she thought about Aunt Robin and Zukah. Both of them would have been able to understand what she was saying, that she was not mentally ill, that it was not her imagination. Both of them would be able to be with her, help her melt the ice over her heart and take some of these dung beetle balls away. She felt pain rise in her throat, but swallowed repeatedly to push it down, sensing her mother couldn't take anything else right now.

Just then Samantha and Stephen returned, both appearing impatient. "So what's happening? Are we going into the hotel?" piped Stephen, picking up his bag in readiness. His floral yellow holiday shirt was like a bright spark in the midst of the shadow that had fallen over the family group.

"Uh yes, yes we're ready." Bill was desperate to find a quick resolution to the family's distress. "I'm going to ask at the desk whether they have a spare room for Abigail; that way you girls can have your own room." He glanced at

Jackie; her scowl suggested she was appalled at his decision. *She'll probably tell me I'm being a "puppet to our daughter's insanity."* But then Jackie seemed to drift away, perhaps overloaded. As he led the way to the check-in desk, his wife looked as if she had checked out of the family for a while.

The entrance was cavernous, just as Bill remembered it. The colors were all warm: peachy orange outside, lemon yellow inside. African regalia filled the walls, the blacks, browns and reds in stark contrast to the light spring shades of the walls. An African man greeted them. He was kitted in a navy jacket adorned with small badges from all over the world, clearly gifts from prior guests. His grin was so wide that it appeared to split his face in two, as if it would burst his skin at any moment. "Greetings, welcome to Victoria Falls, let me take your bags." He fetched a trolley, loaded the bags and directed the family over to the check-in counter.

From behind the counter an African woman, her head and body wrapped in bright orange and navy African cloth, watched the white family. She thought they appeared disconnected from each other, as if they were not a unit. "Over here," she beckoned, trying to get their attention.

The man spoke softly, his shoulders hunching over the counter. "I'd like a separate room for my youngest daughter. Is that possible?" the words stumbled out ill-formed from his mouth.

"Well," the woman told him, "we have one room, but it is a long way from your suite. Are you interested in taking that one?" Her face remained neutral, but behind the polite mask she thought, *What a strange culture these whites have, everyone so independent, even in a family!*

The man turned to the adolescent boy in their group. "Stephen, would you feel comfortable in that one, so Samantha and Abigail can be near us?" He looked intently at his son while he leaned over his daughters' bodies in a stance that looked protective.

"Yah, that's OK." The check-in clerk saw the boy's shoulders straighten at the thought of a bit of independence.

"That's settled, then," said the man, looking askance at his wife. But she gave him no nod of approval. In fact, she was looking away as if it were none of her concern. Perhaps, thought the clerk, she was not this family's wife and mother after all, but some guest they'd brought along. She passed the man the keys and watched him hand them out. "Right, then, Stephen, meet here at four and we'll all go on a game drive this afternoon." The man's shoulders drooped visibly under the burden of command, but the woman (whether wife or guest) showed no sign of helping him chart the group's course. If anything, she'd grown even more distant. *He's nearing his limit,* the clerk realized. She watched his departing back for a moment before she turned back to her work.

It was five after four and Bill kept glancing at his watch, anxiously waiting for Stephen in the lobby of the hotel. Jackie and the girls had sprawled out on the wide-backed straw chairs. The jeep was waiting for them by the entrance. He had tried to talk to Jackie about Abigail's earlier conversation, but now the tables were turned; she was the one who closed the topic vehemently as soon as he brought it up. It worried him, and the thought that she would need to take time off work if this continued worried him even more. He was starting to wonder whether she was clinically depressed. In eighteen years of marriage she had never retreated for this long. It was Jackie's style to get into angry conflicts and then retreat for a while. He was used to that, but now he was living with a frozen sea coated in ever-thickening ice.

He knew this was also hurting Abigail, that Abigail felt responsible for her mother's condition. He hadn't had time to process his thoughts about the earlier conversation. For now, he was grateful that Abigail was with the family, spending time in their shared activity and not retreating to the same extent as her mother. He pushed the bizarre details of the conversation from his mind. *I'll make a point of chatting with her later; and help her get a handle on her imagination. That's all she needs,* he reassured himself. *The more I'm able to ground Abigail, the easier it will be for Jackie to relax.* At least he had a plan of action. That always helped him in challenging times. He felt his fingers form fists and push his nails into the palm of his hand as a way of expressing the tension that he sensed filled him nearly to capacity. He looked up and with relief saw Stephen approaching the family. The boy bounced with an enthusiastic gait, yellow shirt flapping in the soft warm breeze.

Chapter 12

The family was packed tight behind the bars in the jeep. Abigail sat upright between her parents in the back seat and tried to laugh at small things, anything to bring lightness to the family right now. Samantha and Stephen crushed together in the front seat next to the driver Tongwe. Samantha's body kept rising up and down as she tried to get comfortable, and she would sigh periodically. The jeep headed out following a road that snaked close to the river. Tongwe explained the route: "We will go to the place where the river is waking up and sit still and wait for game. They like this place. We will see many birds and maybe the *shumbas*; the big cat of Africa will visit the river. It may be our lucky day," he told the children, delighting in the animated expressions on their faces as they anticipated the adventure ahead. He pulled his camouflage cap further over his head, his dark eyes gloating on the world he was about to share. Bill stared out through the bars, trying to ignore the tension he sensed in both Abigail and Jackie. *This is one of my favorite activities,* he remonstrated internally. *Chill, Bill, drink it in—this is Africa at its very best.*

The jeep bounced on the dirt road, veering to avoid the potholes. Bill noticed everyone's eyes on hyperalert as they tried to track any flicker of movement in the bush all around them. The African grasses were the color of an earthy corncob; they were erect with only the tips brushed slightly by the warm breeze that caressed the land. Trees gathered behind the grasses as if they were creating a backdrop for a play devoted to the African wilds. Further in the distance Bill could see the smudged outline of the pale purple hills. *It's perfect,* he thought; the landscape *is beckoning one to give over to spirit and soar.*

"Look there!" Stephen shouted "Lion."

Tongwe brought the jeep to an abrupt stop, and slowly started to wend the vehicle backwards on the dust-filled road. A cloud of dust formed over the jeep, creating a barrier to their vision. Everyone's eyes were peeled back, eager to see the outline of Africa's most revered cat. As the dust began to settle Stephen pointed over to the acacia tree; sure enough a pride of lions lay in the shade, their heads the color of the grasses around them.

"There are five of them," Tongwe whispered. "The shumba are at peace. The sun must fall more before they will move." He turned the car engine off and the whole group sat in a sacred silence. Minutes went by and no one moved or spoke. One of the female lions lifted her head up a little more, straining to see the large foreign shape ahead; but her body and the others' expressed lethargy. Their bodies were spread-eagled as if to devour all of the shade they were under. Their presence was both threatening and awe-inspiring. Bill imagined one attacking the jeep, reaching its claws through the widely spaced bars, tearing at any flesh within reach. He took note of his vivid imagination. *It's clear where Abigail got it from,* he reflected; still, a shiver went through his body. He glanced over, noting Abigail's expression. She looked transfixed. Her eyes were moving from the lions to a space in front of her eyes, back and forth as if she were watching a game of ping-pong. Bill was mesmerized. What could possibly grab her attention as much as the lions? Her passion for wildlife was unbridled. Bill soon lost all interest in the lions, and was intensely focused on his daughter. At one moment he looked up and the glare of his wife's frightened eyes stared at him, haunting the moment with a somberness he hadn't felt in years.

Abigail, unaware of her parents' reactions on either side of her, felt swept up in the moment. The smoke was swirling all around just in front of her eyes and she watched it, and watched the lions, wondering if the smoke was trying to give her a message about the lions. She had never seen the smoke rise and fall repeatedly in chaotic twirls. Was it trying to warn her of something? She put her hands on her head, massaging frantically to create some space. Then faintly and barely perceptibly she heard a voice say in her head: "Move now—otherwise you will face danger." She felt her body stiffen; how on earth was she going to be able to get the family to move? She felt like she was in the middle of a murder mystery and she had just been given a vital clue, but it was hard to feel certain. She felt her head swim around in a vortex of confusion and self-doubt, but part of her managed to hold on. Her mind focused on the idea that there appeared to be coordination between the smoke and the voice in her head. She didn't know whether to be frightened or relieved by this realization; there was a constant flow of new experiences, as if she had arrived on a new planet on her own, and was starting to piece together vital information about different ways of living. She sensed she was living way beyond her years, like an intrepid pioneer, trying to enlighten those around her who were receptive to ideas that were foreign, frightening and extraordinary. Suddenly she came back to the moment and remembered the strong warning in her mind. She blurted out, "Can we go now? I want to see the river." Her body rocked back and forth with worry.

"Just hold on, Abigail," Stephen responded in an irritated tone. "We're all still watching."

Bill's leg moved up and down. He tried to still it, but to no avail. He was transfixed by the expression on his daughter's face; this was evidence that she was watching something invisible to him. He looked over to Jackie once more, but she had turned her head as if this was a world she did not want to take part in.

After Abigail's request, Tongwe put his head down for a moment; he was curious about the intense feelings expressed by the young girl. His gut instinct was that the girl might have picked up on imminent danger. He started the car in spite of the boy's resistance and jerked the car into action. "The girl is right—there may be danger. We should move now." His voice was adamant.

As the vehicle rolled forward he pulled down hard on the steering wheel, intuitively driving as far over to the right as possible. Up ahead he saw the road meander close to the dam's edge. A little further ahead he noticed a group of hippos move their bodies out of the water and head toward the road. Tongwe sensed the danger; the jeep was low on the ground and the hippos could charge through the bars of the vehicle with stupendous force. He stepped his foot flat on the foot pedal. The jeep jerked, and the family went into silent high alert. No one spoke or moved; all were able to see the formidable grey shapes poised on top of stubby, grey table ends, moving their heaving frames speedily toward the road at a miraculous speed. The jeep, careening at an intense clip, arrived at the closest point to the animals. The road sliced through the dam on a low bridge, closing off the animals' access to the larger part of the dam. The gargantuan hippo closest to the edge lunged forward, narrowly missing the back of the jeep. Bill watched Tongwe's hands on the steering wheel. His grip was firm and implied strength, but creamy smudges were evident underneath his knuckles.

"We are lucky," Tongwe exhaled loudly. "The hippo knows God has given him the biggest mouth and he can eat what he likes. Today we were helped by your daughter's wisdom."

Bill looked over to Abigail and then to Jackie. "Well done, Abigail—how did you know there was going to be danger?" Jackie turned away again as soon as he asked the question, as if anything Abigail said now would be traumatic for her and she wanted to block it out. Her face was pale, her jaw clenched, and it appeared as if she was willing some force to take her away, away from all this distress to a world where she could retrieve her identity.

Abigail noticed her mother's reaction. She sensed any talk about the smoke and the voice might push Mom over the edge. "I dunno, Dad, it was just a feeling." Her hands rubbed her thighs repeatedly as if she could iron out her mother's anxiety.

"Hey, Dad, did you see how close that hippo got? He nearly bashed into us!" Stephen shouted excitedly.

"I saw his eye, that's how close he was," Samantha said her voice matching Stephen's pitch.

"As Tongwe says, we're very lucky. Good for you, Abigail, and thank you Tongwe for following your intuition, too. You both have literally saved our lives today. That could have been ugly. I've heard the hippo is especially dangerous if one gets in between a hippo on the bank and the water. The car was blocking off the rest of the dam; it must have seen that as very threatening. Is that why it charged, Tongwe?" Bill questioned.

"Sir, you are right, the car was threatening its path to the other side of the dam. This is the first time the hippo has charged me in this area. The hippo is a big spirit. If I see him in the river, I pray to God; he has the power to take my life, I know that. I never go looking for the hippo; many tourists ask me, 'Take me to the hippo.' I think these people don't understand the hippo. They don't know he is the chief of the water, along with the crocodile."

Tongwe took a left turn and the new road followed the Zambezi. Bill spotted glimpses of the river through the trees. "Is this where the river wakes up, Tongwe?" Bill asked, noticing a group of guinea fowls scuttling into the bush. "Guineas, everyone; look at their spotted feathers."

"Where, Dad?" shrieked Samantha. "I love guinea fowl!"

"Just over there. Look, you can still see their blue heads in the bush." Bill leaned forward, craning his neck to take in the birds fully. Tongwe slowed down the car so the family could see the frenetic birds chatting away to their group with their distinctive clicks.

"Yes, there they are," Samantha joined in again. Trying to include her mother (who looked as if she had taken a trip to some other galaxy), she added, "Mom, look at their cute heads."

"Did you see them, Jackie?" Bill asked, sensing the deep fog all around her. *She looks so far away,* he thought. *My wife of eighteen years has become a stranger to me.* He felt a pang in his heart as he admitted it to himself.

"Uh, what did you say, Bill?" Jackie looked up, brushing her hair aside in an attempt to be present.

"Oh, not to worry, Jackie; it was just a group of guinea fowls," Bill said feeling deflated by her distancing.

"I'm still thinking about the hippo," she said. "That really shook me up."

Well, at least she's letting us in a little, thought Bill, looking over and observing the woman next to his daughter as if she were a foreigner in the car. He felt the sadness again, wondering if he would ever get his wife back. *I'm not a psychologist,* he thought to himself, *but she looks traumatized every time Abigail lets her imagination go wild. Why can't she just view it like me? Why does she have to put Abigail in a box with a label, and then worry excessively that her life is going to be spent in a mental institution?*

But when Bill thought some more, he realized how much information he had blocked out: the conversation on the tarmac, the lion scene and Abigail's eye movements. He felt his own worry build. That conversation was really bizarre. He questioned himself, searching for clues to explain her prediction of danger, and her watching something so fervently that clearly wasn't there. As for vehemently requesting a single room to talk to spirits, that was psychiatric for sure. Confusion and bewilderment started to erode some of his peace. Maybe he was the one in denial, and maybe this was really serious. Could Abigail have schizophrenia after all? After a while he didn't know what to think; he played frantically with the change in his pocket while staring out at the river. Jackie looked over with a scowl but he didn't notice. *What can I do to fix it?* he pondered repeatedly. *There must be something I can do to fix this situation.*

"We will stop here," Tongwe commanded, pulling the jeep under a mopane tree with its distinctive butterfly-shaped leaves. The dust on the road started to settle, layers followed other layers, gravity pulling their ghostlike red breath to the earth. Tongwe indicated the start of the fenced path to the hide.

Bill walked behind, wanting to be sure that the gate was locked behind them. He felt like a sheepdog rounding up and protecting the sheep in his flock—this family couldn't take anything else; the hippo incident had been too much. His eyes followed Jackie and Abigail. Jackie looked frail, with her slim frame in khaki pants and a lavender t-shirt hugging her waist, her shoulders hunched as she drifted down the path with a robotic gait. Abigail walked in her shadow, unconsciously, he thought, trying to be close to her. *Jackie doesn't realize how desperate her daughter is to make contact.* Bill walked a little faster, catching up to put his arm on Abigail's shoulder. He squeezed it, letting her know he was here; he could be the oak tree that she could lean on.

He loved his children equally. Nothing was more important for him than his role as a father. Some men went into fatherhood with reluctance, hoping they would adapt to it somehow. He, on the other hand, had been dedicated and enthusiastic from the beginning. He remembered reading all about childbirth before the children were born, and coaching Jackie during labor. He was fascinated by the developmental stages, and would read them periodically if he felt he couldn't relate to their present struggles. He encouraged them to read poetry and recite more lines than was expected for their age group so their minds would excel. He would take them out in the bush and try to excite their curiosity in the natural world. Both he and Jackie paid attention to their natural talents, and offered them classes in any area of interest.

Clearly Samantha was the artist; anything she put her mind to turned into a piece of art whether she was painting, sculpting, designing clothes or making batiks. Her eyes were so refined that she could see imperfections or beauty in objects around her that others didn't see. He felt good about her going to art classes, and about the family's support for her obvious talent.

Stephen's love of horses had also been encouraged by his riding lessons. On a horse, he looked as if he had entered another world, as if he had been born on a horse, their spirits attached by some invisible thread from centuries ago.

Abigail was the intuitive one. She had also historically been the socialite, but not now, he concluded, squeezing her shoulder again. He didn't want any loathsome young man taking advantage of her innocent and trusting spirit in the future. He had always felt comfortable with her hanging out with Zukah. Sure, he was a young man, but upstanding, so sensitive in his mannerisms, so respectable in his conduct. *I must study Shona culture,* he reflected; *maybe it would help in some way with our present struggles with Abigail.* For now, though, he was going to put it all out of his mind and just focus on much-needed family time together. Yes, that was part of the solution, he affirmed to himself, noting his shoulders feeling lighter than before.

The family crouched down as soon as they got to the hide, sitting on the low rustic bench as quietly as possible. The sun, now descending in earnest, was a ball of molten orange and red. It appeared determined to put on a memorable light show before its disappearance. Orange tendrils sprayed out, touching all plant life in their view. As the light caressed the branches and the grasses, it gave the impression that their tips were on fire. The red then mixed in with the orange, increasing the intensity of the colors so they burned even brighter. The orange and red mix played in the river, chasing the forms that were merging and reemerging in a quixotic dance. Though the sky invited peaceful slumber, the river raced ahead. Eddies and whirlpools formed in the middle of the river, and water splashed over the rocks with enthusiasm, leaving spraying rivulets of bright white. *Tongwe is right,* thought Bill; *the river has woken up.* It was as if its soul now knew where to go and was determined to race to its destination, picking up strength along the way. He imagined his family, uncertain of its path, getting trapped in the bulrushes alongside the river because it had not yet woken up; they had felt some turbulence, then instead of riding it out had fearfully retreated to the false security of the static bulrushes. Retreating, he reflected, was part of the human condition, a putting off of the inevitable. Perhaps one needed to be tossed around in an eddy or two before one could find the current. Then one could flow down the river with enthusiasm and success. He liked that image; this river was giving him strength. The family was now in the bulrushes building their courage and at a later date would be ready to take on the turbulence, and learn together to surf the rapids; then, more certain of their direction, they would have all the strength, direction and momentum they needed for the next phase of their journey together.

Bill looked around and saw all eyes scrutinizing the land above the river-bank, searching for any wildlife that had come to the river to drink. Nothing moved, only the river. The family and Tongwe sat in pregnant silence, temporarily soothed by nature's light show. Suddenly a shriek was heard from the sky above and an African fish eagle, enormous wings spanning the sky, swooped down into the river. In slow motion it tucked in its feet, its wings folded like curtains as it hovered over the rushing water. Then an effortless dip, its claws poised, and it flapped again, securing a large fish steadfastly between its tawny talons. Its wings now flapped furiously as it ascended; a resounding "kow, kow, kow" let loose like a solo instrument in the orchestra, each note sung with the intensity of victory.

"Wow," Bill said in hushed tones, feeling the rush of the wilderness all around him. As the last note of the fish eagle echoed over the river, Bill heard the mélange of twitters and piercing notes all around. Tongwe then waved his hand to catch the family's attention and pointed over to the riverbank. A group of zebras had their mouths in the water. Some looked around skittishly for lurking predators. A little later, some bucks came through the dense foliage, nudging their small heads out in the open before moving forward. This was Africa, thought Bill; furtive, aware, awake and ever-present; no wonder he felt so alive and at peace here. It was like being part of a drama, the play at any time taking drastic turns, with unpredictability in charge, and every moment exploding with life.

Tongwe beckoned patience with an arm gesture. Bill sensed he was aware of something lurking behind the trees on the other side of the bank. In a couple of minutes there was a crackling sound, and tree branches swayed back and forth to herald the arrival of a large wild animal. The family froze in anticipation. Soon a head appeared and the zebras and bucks reacted instantly, pounding their feet along the bank and veering into any openings in the foliage, their feet suspended like dancers before they tucked away into the green expanse. The buffalo's horns appeared first, two distinctive white circles pointing back threateningly to its own skull. Its eyes peered ahead; as if it had sensed there was company in the distance, it lifted up its head to sniff its surroundings. No one in the hide moved, all of them in awe of the sight ahead. After a while the buffalo seemed to give up on its investigations and slowly moved its tawny frame, splotched with mud patches, closer to the water's edge and stooped to drink. Bill took in its formidable form—so much strength, as if it were an anchor in the chaos of the African wilds. *That is my role for Abigail and Jackie*, he reflected. *I will be a buffalo in the storm of our family lives; I will hold my ground, state my presence with firmness so that those who are off-center around me can draw from my strength.* After a while the buffalo sidled along the bank. No matter at which angle Bill scanned its body, each view denoted an awesomely grounded power. Slowly it moved back into the dense trees and shrubs, taking white egrets with it on its back, their spindly legs holding on tightly to the lumbering beast below.

Tongwe looked over to the group, saying quietly, "Africa will always surprise us—let us wait a while until the sun leaves the day."

Bill nodded, gesturing approval for all of the family. "We will wait patiently, Tongwe," he replied. He looked at his family next to him. All were watching a wildlife movie, their eyes still focused on the bank ahead. Silence hovered like a ghost among them, enveloping their spirits in a shroud. It seemed ages to Bill, but likely it was only ten minutes or so before some small fawn-colored duikers moved onto the bank. Their rubberlike legs looked ready to propel their bodies into the air and away from any danger. Bill counted six of them—he noticed their furtive movements, as if they knew their world could change drastically in milliseconds. One appeared to lead the group, and it moved toward the bank of the river. Feet splayed, it slowly dipped its head into the water closest to the edge, and the others followed tentatively. Then, with absolutely no warning, a striking tail whipped the river water; and at the same instant an enormous gladiator-head emerged, jaw wide open, and clamped down on one of the duikers' necks. Blood spewed out onto the bubbling river, the red dye swallowed instantaneously by the water. Glaring evidence remained; Bill sensed the family cringing at the gruesome sight of the duikers limp body dangling from the crocodile's wide mouth. Bill hadn't noticed when the other duikers had fled. Now the crocodile slowly moved its fearsome body around, prey trapped in its jaws, and pointed its long head and nose toward the river. It started to submerge with the duiker until only its tail slid along the river bank, creating furrows in the wet sand as it pushed all of itself into the gushing water.

"Aah, it is the nature of Africa: Eat or be eaten. It is the way of the bush," Tongwe murmured, aware of the family's shock. "The grasshopper that sleeps forgetfully wakes up in the mouth of the lizard."

"That duiker was really young," Abigail added, voice shaking with feeling.

"Yes, why didn't it go for an older one, Tongwe?" Samantha asked.

"The crocodile is clever," Tongwe replied. "He will go for the one that he can capture with ease. The young ones are the most vulnerable and the easiest to catch. He is Chief of the river, along with the hippo."

"I hate crocodiles," Samantha declared. "They look evil."

"Me, too" Abigail followed. "Where will it take the duiker?"

"Aah, the crocodile needs the body to de-compose before he eats it. He will take the duiker to his den in the river and leave it there for some time before he eats it. This is the way of the master of the river," Tongwe said gently, his mellifluous voice soothing the family. Tongwe stood up; his frame was tall and lean in the standard khaki green ranger attire. "It is time for us to go before the night takes over the day. We have had many experiences in the bush today; we have been lucky."

The family followed Tongwe; Jackie moved slowly behind the children and Bill followed up in the rear. Bill walked a little faster and put his arm around Jackie's slim frame. "How are you doing?" he asked as gently as possible.

"I'm tired, Bill, that's all. I'm tired." She pulled away as if preferring to stay in her bubble.

Abigail heard her mother's voice and turned around instantly, then, stooping, she slowly turned back. Guilt flooded her insides. *It's my fault Mom looks so scared and unhappy. If I hadn't told her about the smoke and voices she would be her normal self.* Abigail hung her head down, feeling ashamed that she had withdrawn heavily on her family's stability account. *Why can't I just be happy like everyone else?* she admonished. *Why do I have to bring up such difficult things to hear?* Internally she made a pact: *I will keep silent from now on; I will not talk to anyone about what I see or hear, only the spirit at night.* Without Zukah and Aunt Robin, the spirit was her only friend, her only true ally in a dizzying world of confusion and loneliness.

Chapter 13

The grandfather clock on the wall said eight-twenty. The family sat around the breakfast table in the hotel's vast dining room. The walls were pale green, each a tribute to African art. One wall had a collection of Makishi masks, a local tribe; the largest mask portrayed a red skull, cheeks painted in the traditional colors of red, white and black. The beard was made of straw and convincingly hung down like Rastafarian matted hair. Bill marveled at African art; he loved the way the cultures honored the natural world in their designs. It was so different from Northern Ireland, where he would need to visit an art gallery to admire the range of local talent. Here it was more like living art, art expressed in dress, dance, masks, tablemats, crockery, candles, batiks, paintings, and carvings of wood and stone. *Art is let loose in this society,* he reflected, *unbridled, just as it should be, not sequestered in some remote shop somewhere.*

The aroma of eggs, bacon and toast brought him back to the table. He looked around and took in the family rabble. Stephen appeared high-spirited, his cheeks flushed and his grin a little wider than usual. Always chipper, that boy, a low-maintenance child who just got on with his life, kept up his studies, had fun with his pals. He had always been like that, Bill reflected, uncomplicated, the polar opposite of Abigail. Samantha also looked good, he thought. Her hair was a little tidier, less of it covering her eyes like a horse's mane; her eyes looked bright as if her senses were on high alert. She needed more attention than Stephen, but she was content with her own company, not needing all the external stimulation Abigail did.

He remembered how complicated he had been in his childhood, always questioning. His sisters, he recalled, would roll their eyes and say under their breath, *"so deep, Bill is always so deep."* In that way he could relate to Abigail: he, too, had been inclined toward philosophical ponderings most of his life. He had always felt he had swum outside the fish bowl, having a perspective that others didn't have. His lens was more critical, less accepting of some of the propaganda he read in the newspapers. Friends and colleagues would encourage him to lighten up, just as his family used to. How could he, especially when he saw through the shenanigans? How could he keep his lips sealed? This characteristic had won him both friends and enemies; some people admired his ability to hold his ground when others felt obliged to agree. He had watched his father serve groceries in his store to both the Catholics and Protestants in Northern Ireland. His father took a lot of heat for going against the tide of bigotry, so it felt natural for Bill to swim upstream, speak his truth no matter the consequences. Honesty was one of his most cherished values; no one could persuade him there was such a thing as a white lie. A statement was either a lie or it wasn't; in his book this "white" business was just a convenient manipulation to handle guilt.

Bill hesitated before he could bring himself to rest his eyes on Jackie and Abigail. He stared instead at the saltcellar; gathering strength from another form of African creativity before he looked up. Jackie looked down as soon as he met her eyes. They had chatted before they went to bed about the duiker and crocodile, but as soon as he had mentioned the family she'd yawned and headed for bed. Bill's goal of communicating closeness and opening a conversation had eluded him as she had curled up far away from him.

Bill moved his eyes over to Abigail. Her brown t-shirt brought out her color and her tanned skin, but her eyes looked heavy. He noticed fine black lines underneath them that made her appear serious and melancholy, as if she were carrying a backpack of worry on her shoulders. He felt his heart ache over her fragility; in her pain and confusion, he saw the most vulnerable part of himself. His tender, sensitive family philosopher … How could he save her from herself? He knew instinctively she would have many humbling lessons in life; such was her path. Other than support her and bear witness, he would be helpless; he could not take the lessons away.

He felt overwhelming determination to try to cheer everyone up, to try desperately to uplift Abigail and Jackie's spirits. "Well, who's keen to go Chongololo hunting at the falls today? Whoever finds one first gets the biggest ice cream!"

"OK, Dad," piped up Stephen, "Hey, I'm great at finding Chongololo—bet I'm going to win. I won the last time and got five dollars extra in pocket money."

"Samantha and I are good, too, Stephen, so don't think you're going to win," Abigail said, tentatively seduced by the challenge.

"We'll see about that," Stephen said, eating his fried eggs hurriedly, with some of the egg landing back down on his plate.

"Don't talk with your mouth full, Stephen and you're using your fork like a shovel," Bill scolded; it was one of his pet peeves.

"Mmmm," Stephen mumbled back, quickly eating the remaining food in his mouth. "Samantha was doing it too, and you never spoke to her about it."

"No I didn't," Samantha replied, making sure her mouth was free of food before she spoke.

Bill glanced over at Jackie and saw the irritation evident in her frown and tight lips. "OK, that's enough," silencing the dispute before it could become an argument. "We're going to have a brilliant day at the Falls, so eat up. Then we can catch a taxi and go."

The children responded immediately; they knew not to push their father's tolerance. All three heads focused on their food below, their forks and knives clicking on their plates as the last of their meal was consumed.

Abigail looked around once she was finished. There were three other families eating at the same time. The family next to their table had two young daughters, about her age, she thought, sitting with their parents. Everyone looked relaxed. The color of their clothing was bright and it seemed to match their spirits. *Our family seems so serious right now! We never used to be like this.* She looked at her mother in her navy top and her father in his dark brown t-shirt. Only Stephen wore bright colors; the rest of them were in muddy green, brown and navy, as if to illustrate the dark worry in their group. Abigail glanced over again and saw how casually the mother was seated in her chair. She was attractive, with short blonde hair and pale green eyes, but it was her smile that really captivated Abigail. She couldn't remember when she last saw her own mother smile like that, light and breezy, as light as dust trailing behind a car, rising and falling gently and freely. That other mother looked so contented.

Abigail wondered when her family became so serious and worried; she felt a large dung beetle ball move over to the center of her brain, taking up enormous space. *I need to figure this out!* She was angry at the dung beetle balls; they had taken charge of her life. Every time she wanted to sort through her confusion, they took over and made it impossible. The list of what she needed to sort out kept getting longer. She hadn't yet figured out why the smoke over the dog had followed her home. She didn't know why she could hear a voice in her head, especially at night when the house was quiet and everyone was asleep. She felt overwhelmed still at what had happened a couple of days ago, when the smoke and the voice had seemed to be giving the same warning. How could the smoke coordinate with the voice in her head? Was she going mad, was her mother right? Maybe she did have a mental illness, the one with a long name starting with an S. She didn't feel normal anymore; if you couldn't talk about what you were experiencing then maybe that did mean you were going crazy. Fear began to rise; she could feel it in her throat.

What would her life be like if she went completely mad? Would her mother still talk to her? Already conversation was very short. What about her father? Would he be able to accept that the "family philosopher" had gone mad? She had heard of men from the war going mad; a friend had told her a story of a young man who had shot himself because of the war and all that he saw. Maybe going mad was related to what you saw in the world, and whether you could find people to talk to about your experience. *I'm the only one I know that sees smoke and hears a spirit in my head. Will I be able to be grown up if I'm crazy? Will this keep me from getting married and having children? Will people just ignore me my whole life? Will my family still love me?* The questions crashed into her mind like a river increasing its velocity, filling every crevice, worming into all the corners and subterranean channels. She felt it, she felt the confusion as a blanket snuffing out the air. Thought became impossible, and her sense of self was eroding. She felt her spark, her vitality vanishing along with the air. *I'm never going to be the same again,* she mourned.

Loneliness rose like a volcano about to spew, and sadness welled in her heart. *No one will ever understand me again,* she concluded, letting go even more of the overwhelming wish to be close to her mother again. Her mother had been turned into a shadow (*just like me*, Abigail thought), drifting in and out of the family's lives, barely there. It was too painful to look at her mother's face again, so Abigail kept her head down and stared at the empty plate. It reflected back the void she felt inside; it was a comfort, somehow. She felt as if she were recoiling into a dark solitary world where few would be able to make meaningful contact with her.

She recalled now her mother and father got a lot more serious when she talked about the voices in her head. She suddenly recoiled from the memory of her parents discussing "her illness" and from the loneliness she had felt from that day on. If her parents weren't on her side, who could be? She obviously couldn't trust anyone at school anymore; she flinched at the thought of what she felt every day at school. Not even geography was enjoyable these days; there seemed to be little escape. Madeline was still ignoring her and even Rick had cooled. *It's like everyone knows that I'm a freak of some sort, that I don't fit in, that I'm weird and mentally ill.* She reflected on the impact on her siblings; it hadn't affected them as much as it had her parents, although Samantha didn't laugh as much, and Stephen was keeping more to himself. *So it's my fault after all,* Abigail concluded. *I am the problem for this family; it's my strange experiences that have affected everyone.* Guilt and self-loathing washed over her; she felt it going into every pore in her body and taking up permanent residence.

I hate myself, she thought. *I've made so many problems! Look what I've done to my mother.* She mustered all of her courage forcing herself to take in what she had done to her mother. Slowly Abigail glanced up. She felt her eyes squinting as they would in the glare of the sun. It was too painful to take in her mother's face fully; but she felt she needed to face what she had done to her. As she looked at her mother's face she felt the pain inside hurting her heart, like something heavy pressing against it. Her mother's eyes looked hollow, as if they had retreated away from her face and gone to a darker place. Abigail also noted her lips; her mouth was frozen tight. Abigail looked down again, feeling too much. Tears welled up in her eyes, but she blinked, forcing them back. She mustn't let anyone know about her hurt and guilt; only the spirit could understand her now.

She had asked the spirit the night before if it was her fault about her family. The spirit had told her that she must trust herself and that she had gifts for the family and that she was a good person. How could she believe that, when the evidence of her impact was so glaring? This was the one time the spirit got it wrong, maybe because it saw things from a different view; but Abigail knew what she felt was true. Her heart felt heavy, and her head hung like ripened fruit on a thin branch.

Her father noticed. "What's up, Abigail? You look worried."

Mom looked down as soon as she heard Dad's question. Abigail saw her reaction, and knew her mother was blocking out the sound. "Oh, nothing, Dad," Abigail replied, pushing her plate away in hopes that the scrape of the plate on the table would provide a distraction.

"You look upset, Abigail," he said, his voice nurturing and protective.

"I'm OK, Dad," she coughed, trying to muffle the tremor in her voice. *Snap out of it,* she told herself, feeling a mask slip over her soul like thin gauze, separating her public face from the dark turmoil within. She felt lighter, but less herself. *This is how I'll cope; I won't be myself anymore when I'm with others. It's only with the spirit and Zukah that I can be myself,* she concluded, pleased that at least she had sorted something out, despite all the confusion.

"Well, let's go and find those Chongololo." Bill responded, relieved not to have another drama on his hands. The family left the dining room, Abigail trailing behind, and climbed into the taxi that would transport them to the Falls.

At the entrance hung a curved wooden sign stating in understated simplicity "Victoria Falls." *This is what I love about Africa,* Bill thought: *none of the glitz, orange and red neon lights, or over-the-top commercialism I've found everywhere else in the world.*

"Remember everyone, whoever finds the Chongololo first gets the biggest ice cream," he shouted as the children scurried down the path.

The jungle formed on either side and over the pathway like an arch of wild foliage. Trees and shrubs were tangled together in a constricted dance of nature. Vines caressed tree trunks and branches hung carelessly in a dense entanglement of green tendrils. Mist hung in the clammy hot air, an early warning sign of the glory to come. The jungle hummed with life. Cicada beetles released a high-pitched note that declared their presence all around, drowning out some of the bird songs. The family's senses were heightened— this was wild Africa; anything could happen anytime. Sure, they were away from crocodiles and hippos, but lions could move into the area. Snakes, too, were always sneaking and slithering in their perfect camouflage; their venomous heads were often spotted too late to avoid a strike. Danger and mysticism were interwoven in the jungle, making each moment alive with possibility and adventure.

The sound of thunder started to get louder. Bill loved it; *nature's drum,* he thought. The rocks were the base of the drum, and the pounding surf the hand that dropped down on the skin. Bill listened more closely to hear the thunder's echo. A bold boom layered onto a more plaintive grumble, like a conversation between angry titans. The mélange of sound reverberated in Bill's ears, transporting him.

Soon the family could see the clearing up ahead. The blue sky hovered over Devil's Gorge like a blanket, intensifying the contrast between the green jungle and the madly dancing white surf. The family stood mesmerized. A small thorn bush was all that stood between them and a long plummet to death. No one spoke. Each tried to drink in the beauty all at once, but it was impossible. Bill wondered which area inspired the greatest awe. Was it the rainbow arcing and piercing into the gorge below like a multicolored spear of light? Was it the water frothing excitedly over the edge of the cliff and gushing to freefall? Perhaps it was the mist, the gatekeeper of the view, shrouding or exposing the landscape from moment to moment as it rose and fell. Bill fixed his eyes on the river below, on the swirling water and the sharp-edged cliffs that forced the river into tight corners and a narrow passage. Mist rose and fell over the river and the rainbow's arc burned brightest down below. Bill felt his body respond to the beauty; he collapsed into it, surrendering his entire being to nature's glory, imagining every cell of his body being refreshed by his experience. *This is making me stronger. I can feel it!*

After some time, the family followed the path leading to the opening, where the entire falls could be witnessed. Stephen led the way, his pace quickened by anticipation. No one was talking, and Samantha and Abigail's heads were craned, as if their heads could get there faster than their bodies. Suddenly Stephen stopped. Jackie looked up and instantly halted, her body pulling back from the edge of danger. Bill stepped forward and realized they had arrived at the view; Stephen stood there seemingly unable to move. Bill looked at the Zambezi pushing its way over the cliff, moving determinedly past the islands of brush and green shrubs before freefall, clouds of swirling virgin white foam and mist rising up through the cavern, then greeting the effervescent surf with their wispy presence. In places the mist rose valiantly above the land, swirling gleefully before its descent. Bill looked down—adrenalin rushed through his body as he imagined following the foam in a suicidal plunge. Grey granite rocks speared the gushing liquid as it crashed over them, separating it into competing streams of sparkling bubbles. Words and phrases, all inadequate, formed loosely in Bill's mind: "Magnificent wonders," "out-of-this-world beauty," "unimaginable splendor." Beside him, his family stood gaping, similarly short of vocabulary. Even Jackie looked mesmerized. For ages they all stood there, speechless, motionless, surrendering to the fine mist that formed a layer of moisture on their exposed skin.

Eventually Abigail looked up and beckoned to her father to get a glimpse of the rocks from her angle. Abigail kept looking up, for the smoke had appeared as soon as they were out of the clearing. It was dancing with the mist, and they were colliding together in a mystical duet. Abigail wanted her father to put his arms around her; she wanted his protection.

Bill sensed her vulnerability. She seemed more fragile than usual, her small body kitted in her muddy brown shorts and t-shirt. Her tiny frame stood in contrast to the mighty falls; she was swallowed up in the mist, the water rising way above her head. Bill put his arm around her and felt her collapse into his side, as if leaning into a soft, velvety cushion. He held firm; he would anchor her all he could while she moved through the storms of her life. He squeezed her shoulder, silently reassuring her that they would all hold on through the turbulence and rapids, and that all would be well in the end.

Chapter 14

Zukah watched the dancers, transfixed by their lithe bodies moving fluidly to the drumbeat. Their firm legs, effortlessly following the rhythm, poked like long, black snakes from under their short and colorful skirts. Zukah stared at their bare breasts, moving up and down like balls on a string. The fire was the backdrop to their dance. Firelight licked their bodies, illuminating some parts while leaving other parts in shadow. Zukah felt drawn to their bodies like a moth to a bright light. One woman caught his attention. His eyes started to follow her; he felt them squinting as he tried to make out more of her body. He knew her name was Taona. She was older than him but she was still a teenager, maybe eighteen or nineteen, he guessed. Her body seemed different from the rest for some reason. He felt drawn to it—just watching her was creating heat in his body. His head followed her breasts; they were circling and seemed to be communicating with him. He sensed a sensation in his groin and his hands felt restless. He wanted to cup her breasts in his hands, feel them smooth under his skin, and squeeze them between his fingers.

Zukah hadn't felt these urges so intensely before; he had watched many dancers but somehow tonight was different. He looked up furtively, wondering if Taona had seen him watching her. The fire lit up her face; he saw the streaks of sweat pasted on her cheeks, her eyes soulful and shy as if retreating. Then their eyes met through the half-light. Now her body turned around; she had her back to him as she faced the fire. He could see her bottom churning, one cheek moving up and then the other, her legs open, her skirt just covering her private parts. He stared, wondering if more would be revealed. He stared at her back; even her back was alluring. The way it shaped near her bottom, it too had sweat on it. He wanted to put his hand between her legs, feel her private parts. Zukah became aware of his penis stiffening, he had felt this before, but the sensation hadn't lasted. He felt it push up

113

against his trousers as if it were trying to escape and follow its impulses. Taona was now dancing alongside the other women. She moved her hand up to her waist, then higher. Her left hand brushed against her breast. It excited him; he wanted desperately to cup her body there. The drum started to beat more slowly; the dancers started to move out of the circle and make way for the other dancers, who were dancing a more mournful movement near the trees. He remembered his uncle Temba telling him about desire: "Where the heart longs to be the path never reaches."

Zukah knew Taona's dance was celebrating the return of Temba's spirit to his people. He knew, too, that the entire village was aware that he would be a vessel for Temba, and that the dancing was preparation for the Kurova guva ceremony tomorrow. Zukah craned his neck, trying to see the dancers moving under the trees, trying to make out Taona's form. It was impossible; their bodies had formed shadows around the tree. The other dancers now moved closer to the fire. They too had bare breasts, but Zukah didn't feel the same sensation in his body. Their bodies expressed mourning; their shoulders were rounded, their breasts calm and their legs slow. His body shifted, and he felt his penis subside as the excitement left his groin. He started to notice some of the other villagers' faces; one older woman was wiping tears away and burying her face in her hands. He looked for his mother and sister Della—they were huddled next to his father, their faces pained in mourning. He scanned the circle for Temba's wife and children. At first he couldn't see them in the dark, and then he noticed a woman. Her body was scrunched up, her knees were touching her chest, and her children were on either side of her, nestled into her body. Tears were rolling down her face so quickly that she didn't bother trying to smudge them away. Her children looked lost, lost in their mother's grief, lost in the world without their father to guide them with love and wisdom. Zukah felt their pain, along with his own. It felt like drowning from the inside. Their pain and his pain were merging and filling his body with an ache. The mourning dancers intensified the somberness of the occasion; he was surprised how quickly his mood had shifted from lust and excitement to grief.

A calabash of beer was passed among the villagers. He took a sip and passed it on, swirling the liquid around his mouth and celebrating that Temba would be coming back. He felt comforted by the idea that Temba would live through him. He was honored, his family was honored and he knew the village would treat him differently. What he said from now on would be taken very seriously; he realized in some ways he would no longer be a child. This was a big responsibility; he also had the job of finding the snake man in the village, so that harmony could be brought back to the rudzwi again.

The next day his father approached him "Zukah, we are preparing to go to Temba's grave, we are waiting for you," Josef commanded. He was eager to reconnect with his brother through Zukah.

"I am coming, father." Zukah soon joined his family and Temba's on the path leading to the gravesite. His father carried a broom made of straw and a long stick. He handed Zukah a calabash of beer, encouraging him to hold it carefully lest it spill. Busi, Temba's daughter, looked on hyperalert; she carried a wooden plate of different foods and her sister's plate was full of *sadza*. Everyone knew today was the day that Temba would return to his rudzwi through Zukah. Busi appeared impatient with anticipation, her feet ahead of the others, neck craning ahead like an ostrich eagerly seeking sustenance. The jacaranda tree stood tall up ahead. It hovered over Temba's grave and had dropped its lavender petals on the site. The party started to clean the gravesite, pulling out the weeds and brushing aside anything that had fallen on the grave.

Josef then took the beer and poured it on the area, saying in a loud, loving voice, "Temba, it is your family. We have come to take you home. We have missed you, and we are here to help you come back to the rudzwi. Temba Temba Temba," he repeated lovingly. "I am your brother, Josef. Zukah and I are here to serve you." Josef indicated to Temba's daughters to place the plates on the gravesite as an offering. "Drink everyone," commanded Josef "We are here to receive Temba."

The calabash was passed around; everyone took a small sip, holding the gourd in both hands. Busi was the last to partake; then she handed it back to Zukah, smoothing her dress with her hands, her fingers fidgeting all the while.

"Temba is in the tree. I will climb the tree and cut off the branch that Temba is on," Josef declared, following the rituals closely, and talking to the family behind him. Josef wrapped his arms around the trunk, and looked ahead as if something were calling him. Slowly he propelled his large frame up the jacaranda, clinging to a branch. He bent his legs in a froglike fashion, and used his feet on either side to gain traction and push his body upward. After some time he sat on the first branch and pulled his knife out of his back pocket. Slowly he stood up on the branch and leaned on the spine of the tree. Then he started to cut the slim branch above his head. The family members watched in awe, all heads craned to keep their eyes on the spindly branch, knowing Temba must be there. Zukah wondered how his father knew which branch to cut, how he could be sure that Temba's spirit was on the one he chose. Then he remembered: of course, his father would get guidance from the spirit world.

Josef pulled at the branch and it separated from the tree. Quickly Josef grabbed the white cloth on his shoulder and covered the branch, making sure that the spirit would not separate from it. Zukah could hear his father saying, "Temba, it is me, your brother, Josef, Temba it is me, your brother, Josef— we are taking you back home. Please come to guide and protect your family."

Slowly Josef moved down the tree, keeping his right hand upright and away from his body and carefully placing his legs.

As he got to the lowest branch he crouched down. "Zukah, please take the branch, stand close to the tree and take the branch carefully." Zukah reached up and secured the branch in his hand, making sure the cloth remained in place. He handed it back to his father once he was back on the ground. Josef secured the top of the branch under the cloth and dragged the bottom half along the ground. The family followed behind, all captivated in the moment, hearing the drums from the village beating out their arrival. Temba's wife Nyala held her head high, clutching Busi's and her other daughter's hands in hers, proudly walking down the dusty path back to the village.

Zukah hung his head down in deference to the importance of the occasion. He watched the dust moving under others' feet, smothering their toes in red shadows. He imagined the dust to be other spirits joining them, helping their feet to move at the right pace to hold onto Temba. He felt comforted by his culture; soothed by the belief that the loss of a relative did not mean the relationship was gone; it was just a different way of relating. He wanted to be able to see Temba as a spirit; but he wondered whether that was possible. No one had told him what to expect, only that he would be able to access Temba's guidance for himself and his rudzwi, but how would he do that? It was all a mystery, but he concluded that the best things in life were a mystery: Why had he been drawn to Taona's body and not the others? Why did he feel such a comfort around Abigail even though they were different races, living dramatically different lives?

He wondered how white society handled the consequences of death when it was so finite. He wondered also what Abigail thought; did she believe her Aunt Robin was in heaven with God? If she did, she would be very lonely, her soul gutted of meaning, he imagined. He had heard many in white society believed in God and went to church. He wondered how they explained that Mwari the creator, or God, could be so cruel to take away their relatives to be with him and that they would have no contact until their own deaths. You love someone and you take him or her deep into your heart. Then you are supposed to accept they are gone away, and the only comfort you have is to visit a site that holds their crumbling bones. He shook his head at the strangeness of it all, watching the dust at the same time. Life would be empty, meaningless, pointless, he surmised, without spirits around them. They would all be lost; it was such a foreign idea that he could not even imagine it.

Nature was his guide and reservoir of mystery. In Shona culture he knew that the spirits used nature as their medium to express themselves; it was their language. He didn't know how it all worked, but when he saw a go-away bird circling around his head, shrieking its call, he knew it was warning him, and that the spirits had sent the bird. He remembered the time at the river when a small branch of a tree had fallen on his leg while he slept. He had gotten up straight away. About a minute later a crocodile had lurched onto the bank nearby, nose in the air smelling for food. He blessed the spirits for saving him. Then there was the time when his sister nearly stepped on a puff adder; his father had pulled her body to the ground seconds before. His father had told them that his own father had warned him, and told him what to do in that moment. He loved that; he loved the idea that his grandfather could still help them today.

Zukah pondered further: Why do some people not get the help from the spirits when they need them to save their lives? Where was the spirit for Temba when he needed a warning? What about the young girl in the village who died from a sickness; why did the spirits not assist her to get the right medicine? This was a mystery to Zukah; were some without guides or were they not listening, or was it their time to depart from the mortal world? He must ask his father and Uncle Temba about these questions. Now that he had a role in the village, he had to have a deeper understanding of all matters.

He reflected some more: His family, like all the village families, needed help and guidance. Without guidance and help, how would people keep from getting lost? How would they keep from drifting like a log in a river, floating to this bank then to that, not really having direction, just going where the river took them? He had met lost people before; he remembered the white boy, Lucas, Mr. Smithers' son. Zukah remembered the time they spent together. He had tried to connect with him, to get to know him, but it was like water running through his hands; there was nothing to hold onto. He questioned why Lucas had appeared so lost, and concluded he had abandoned his body and heart to live primarily in his head. Thoughts spewed out of him like a river in flood, but there was no connection to feeling.

Zukah recalled an afternoon they'd spent working alongside each other. Mr. Smithers had told his son to do some work in the garden as a punishment, and he didn't know what to do. He had asked Zukah for help, so they had chatted. Afterwards, Zukah had felt confused by his ideas. He was in competition with everyone, it seemed, even his father; he talked of conquering girls, having as many bodies as possible. Zukah remembered it feeling strange that he never mentioned love once. He said he did not like nature; it was something to be disposed of like an old bicycle. He didn't like birds or wildlife; he had said his favorite things were sex and getting drunk. Zukah liked the taste of beer, too, but why would this boy drink so much that he would forget everything? Zukah loved to remember all of the details; he hated forgetting as if he had missed out in some way, as if he had lost some of his life to oblivion. Thinking back to Taona, he could now understand why sex was so powerful for this young man. The urges he had felt in his body had been alarming, but it was Taona he was interested in, not many girls all at once.

His father had only had one wife, and so had Temba. That would change now, as Nyala would now become the second wife of his father, who would become the father to Temba's children. Zukah thought it would feel strange at first. There were many men in his rudzwi that had several wives, but they had chosen that life and it didn't happen through the death of a family member. Maybe they would understand better why the Smithers boy wanted so many women at the same time.

Zukah concluded he was lucky to be born African. *I like white houses and their big gardens, and I'd like to go to school all the time, but what would I do when my mother and father died? My heart would ache for the rest of my life. Also what if I lost my sisters and friends?* At least in his culture, he knew for certain that whoever died he would see on the other side when he died. The separation would be only temporary. Until then, their spirits would be watching over him, helping him, guiding him through intuition. It was hard to lose Temba, but now he would be with him every day, guiding him. This felt right, and he let out a sigh. It was the merging of the living and the dead that made life so mysterious. This was the first time he had not intensely resented being part of a race deemed inferior in his country.

It still angered him that because he was African he could not own certain things, like a house on fertile land. Also to earn money he had to be a slave to the white man. He hated the white government and white people for those ideas. He liked some white people, though; he liked Abigail and her father. *He sees me as an equal to him and his daughter. I still have lots to learn about white people and why they need to feel better than Africans. Maybe Temba will help me with that.* Aah yes, it would be soothing for his soul to have Temba by his side. He wasn't sure how he would experience it, but they would be together; that was all that mattered. At that thought, he looked up and saw the village in full celebration.

The smell of meat cooking was carried on the wind, and Zukah started to salivate. He could hear lots of voices merging with each other, and saw people moving in and out of the circle around the fire, carrying things and bringing items to the center. As he got closer he heard the *mbira*, the African thumb piano being plucked. Its sound melted in his ear and soothed him. The villagers started to hum with the mbira, gently at first, then by the time he neared the circle of people around the fire he heard their voices lifting, harmonizing, melding, and making one sound. Everyone knew the mbira was welcoming Temba home. Their voices ululated with the instrument; the community was together, and the healing had begun. Zukah scanned the circle, feeling the blending of the rudzwi, the togetherness, but as his eyes fell on the thirty or so men in the circle, he wondered which one was the snake. *Temba will tell me soon,* he reassured himself.

Josef took Zukah's hand and led him to the center of the circle, carrying the cloth-covered branch in his hand. The Nechombo and tribal chief stood up and followed Josef to the center. Josef cleared the ground for Zukah with his foot and instructed him to sit next to the fire on the ground. Zukah felt nervous now but he followed the orders. His father, the Nechombo and tribal chief joined hands above him and circled him. He heard unintelligible words—then he felt a wind enter his ear and energy fill his chest. His head felt full suddenly, as if it were going to burst open like a balloon. Then the air began to subside and he felt a warm glow around his heart, and a butterfly flying in his left ear as if it was trapped and couldn't get out. Zukah lifted his hand and pushed on his ear in an effort to release the insect. Josef, and the two elders watched him and smiled. "Temba is home," said the Nechombo; "Temba is home." The crowd heard and suddenly there were wails all around. Zukah heard some crying; others let out a scream as if a wild animal had just been seen; many burst into traditional songs, harmonizing with the mbira. Zukah felt overwhelmed; he was aware that the butterfly was still trapped and didn't know what to do.

His father pulled him up and faced him, cupping Zukah's left ear in his hand. "Temba is with you, my son. His spirit is the butterfly in your ear. Welcome him; he has come home." Josef's pride inflated as he pulled his son to him. *My son Zukah has brought me back my brother; our rudzwi will be well again,* he thought. "From today your name is Temba," Josef bellowed for all to hear, his voice choking with the intensity of the experience.

The next day the two families related to Uncle Temba gathered early in the morning. The sun had begun its rise in the African blue sky and started to envelop the land with a warm glow. Birds heralded the fresh new day, squawking and twittering. They pierced the morning with notes of "Be awake! The morning is here."

"Temba, how are you my son, did you sleep well with spirit?" Josef inquired.

"I slept well, Father. I have not had a message yet. When will it happen?"

"It will happen when it is right. Trust and have faith, my son. His spirit will not let us down, and he is with us now to guide the rudzwi. In time he will help us find the snake in the village. Now it is time for another ritual; we need to communicate with the spirit world."

Josef picked up a calabash of beer from the storage area next to the fire pit, where the village kept their extra grain for the dry season. He then beckoned to the families to follow him. Josef walked solemnly on the path that led to the cattle *kraal*. Until this last ceremony was over, he could not relax fully. His heart was soothed by the thought of his brother being with them, but he wanted assurance from the spirit world that all was aligned.

As they approached, the cattle started to move anxiously in a circle, aware now that they were trapped in a wooden fenced circular pen. The sun shone brightly on their skins, illuminating the creamy and brown blotches.

"I will go in the kraal and put a rope around the bull. I will pull him to this side." Josef indicated the area of the kraal that was covered by an acacia thorn tree, Southern Africa's emblem of wild places. "Temba, have your calabash ready and pour the beer on the bull's head," Josef instructed. The families and women were on high alert; they knew that Josef could have trouble with the bull, and so their silence indicated that their hearts were with him along with their prayers.

Josef pulled up the latch. Tentatively he skirted around the side of the kraal, touching the wood with his hand to anchor him for the task ahead. With the other hand he clutched a rope that he pulled from his waist; he fondled the noose as if willing it to land in the right way. Josef saw the bull in the center; the other cattle were moving nervously around him, sensing that something was about to happen. Some cows started to groan and moo. The families and women could hear Josef muttering to himself unintelligible, soothing sounds. They watched as he stood firm and started to circle the rope around his head. He let it loose and it landed a meter from the bull's head. The bull appeared startled and started to move away to the edge of the kraal. Josef deftly moved to another position and threw the rope up for another try. This time it landed smoothly over the bull's head; Josef quickly pulled it tight so he could secure his hold. The bull started to pull away. Its hooves attacked the ground. Red dust covered its foothold. Josef pulled back his arms, hunching with the strain. Slowly he angled its huge frame around to the area of the fence, closest to the acacia, where everyone was gathered. The bull pulled back and then relaxed as if giving in for a moment. Temba raised his calabash in readiness, and as soon as the bull was close enough he threw it over its head. The bull immediately shook its head and then pushed back against the noose. Instantly the women wailed and the men joined them. Josef dropped the rope and crawled through the middle wooden slat. He stood up proudly, his shoulders back, his head tilted up. "The spirits are happy; the bull has shaken his head. Temba's spirit is happy, too. We can rejoice." Excited sounds melded around him. "Let us return to the village and spread the news that all is well with the spirit world."

The group quickly gathered on the path and started to sing, the sounds melding with the sunlight and lifting their spirits to the heavens. Temba felt his heart was going to burst open with the beauty of it all. His uncle was with him, the spirits were happy, and he would help find the snake so that the village would return to harmony. His life had changed and he felt proud of his new role in the village.

The next morning Temba felt compelled to get up early. His sister Della was sleeping on a blanket on the floor on the other side; always the boys slept on one side and the girls on the other. Two boys from another family were curled up together, like cats lying on each other for warmth. Temba did not want to wake anyone. He slowly maneuvered his body erect, then deftly moved his feet through the opening of the hut. The sun was not up yet, but through the darkness he could see the path in the distance that led to the river. Temba felt his feet move effortlessly, as if a force were pushing his body, compelling him to go to the river. He had not even thought of eating; nothing right now was as important as going to the river. His head was down. He was alone, although he didn't feel alone; but the lack of light frightened him. He could step on a snake in this shadowy light; wild animals could be waking up and moving through the savannah for a kill. The thoughts moved through his mind, but they didn't linger, as if a wind in his head pushed them out.

Temba started to sing to calm himself. "*Vakanga vagere nerunyararo, Vana vechibwe che Zimbabwe,Vachena vakasvika ndokuvaparadzanisa, Vakatanga kutitonga vachititiambudza, Kwakazozvarwa umwe mukomana, Uye ndiye ega ari kuda kutipa rusunungguko, Misodzi nedikita zvinosangana, Weganda dema kana achishanda, Chaanoshandira chisipo, Vana kumusha vanotambudzika.*" ("They were living peacefully, children of the stone of Zimbabwe. The white people arrived and scattered them. They began to rule us in a hard way. Then there was the boy that was born. He is the only one that wants to give us freedom, but the whites do not like this. Sweat and tears mix, when the black man is working, working for nothing; children at home are miserable.")

As Temba was singing he remembered the war had ended. His father had told him that the whites were negotiating with a full black government and the country would now be called Zimbabwe. Soon maybe he could feel like he belonged fully in this country of his birth, not just to certain sections of his world. Maybe he would feel more comfortable in the white man's world, as if he had a place or purpose there, instead of feeling like a dog with his tail between his legs, scurrying around trying not to be noticed. Maybe all of them would feel they had a place everywhere in Zimbabwe, all moving around freely, the chains loosened and spirits set free. He could not trust the white government; only when a black man held permanent power would Temba fully believe their lives had changed.

Temba's pace quickened as he heard the river. The butterfly was now flying in his ear; he put his hand up as if to release it. It was an odd sensation, but comforting, as he knew it was his uncle trying to get his attention. Temba looked all around him; maybe he was being alerted to a wild animal slinking in the bush. Temba felt his eyes bulge out of their sockets, and his heart fluttered in response to the cautionary danger signal. The shadows started to lift off the land like vapors of mist; it looked like the sun was dancing with them first before attempting to burn them away. A glimmer of golden light could be seen on the horizon piercing through the black, spearing it with gold. Temba felt his breath quicken. What was up ahead? Were there lions lurking at the river, ready to leap on top of their prey and sink their sharp teeth into the back of his neck? "Help me, Temba," he whispered out loud.

"Protect me. I know you want me to go to the river, but help me stay alive."
Temba could see the river in full view; he looked instantly for shapes in the
trees beyond, moving shapes. He stood still to observe. His neck craned like
a giraffe, as if those extra inches could make a difference between life and
death. *Why didn't I wait,* he thought, *until it was lighter? I could have asked
my father to come with me.*

Then he answered himself, *I am meant to be here; Temba's spirit has
brought me here.* He took in a deep breath and a sigh went with it. The river
was calming him, even though he knew rivers could be dangerous in the
early morning. Unconsciously he pushed his finger into his ear in an attempt
to calm the butterfly, and calm his thoughts. Temba moved slowly over to the
rocks, peering over his shoulder periodically. The water pulled at him, as if it
had magnetized his feet and was reeling them in closer to its shores. He
followed the sensation, trusting that he was going to be protected no matter
what happened.

The light was now winning over the dark. The sun's glow shone on the
dew on the grass, exposing the moisture clinging on precariously. Temba
took one last look over his shoulder and then sat down on a rock, staring at
the river all the while, his eyes fixated on the part of the river that crashed
around the boulders. The spray bubbled on top of the surface angrily as it
moved furiously down the river. Just then Temba felt his head being pulled
up; he noticed a human form standing on the river. The bubbles submerged
its feet but its body was erect. He could see a man's shape, but as soon as he
was clear about the gender, the form reshaped itself, its shoulders melding
with its torso and then reforming. Temba felt his body go cold. He looked at
the face and saw the cheeks fold into the mouth and then reform. Was it
Temba? He looked harder. The man was taller than Temba and his shoulders
looked hunched as if he were older than Temba.

Am I having a vision? He asked himself. *Who is this person? Am I
supposed to know them?* Just then a thought dropped into his head: *The
snake.* As if jolted by electricity, Temba stood up quickly and moved closer
to the water, hoping to see more clearly, but the shape moved as if it understood his intent. He felt he had a good recollection of the body shape; but it
was the face he was after. The head was small, and the eyes seemed sunken,
and both ears protruded from the skull. The head merged into the neck; but
just before it did he noted the neck was long and slim like that of an ostrich.
The shape appeared to be dancing on the river; the bubbles were its music
and the rhythm of the river its beat. It then turned to the side; Temba looked
again at its face and absorbed the shape of the nose in memory. The nose was
large but it turned up at the end, and on the side was a blob of flesh. The
shape shifted to the other side; and Temba noted again the mound on the side
of the nose. His body relaxed; with the nose, the long neck, the small head
and protruding ears, and hunched shoulders, he was going to be able to

identify the snake man, the one that orchestrated his uncle's death. At that moment the shape suddenly merged into the bubbles and was gone.

Temba glanced up, noting if anything else was around him. Then he heard an African lowrie in the distance: "Goway, goway," it called. Temba knew instantly that an animal was on its way to the river; nature had given him his signal. Quickly he moved back onto the path, his bare feet sensing the fine dust beneath them. His pace was swift but in his heart he felt relaxed. His spirit felt melded with the world around him. *As a vessel for a Mudzimu I am safe,* he reflected; *and I now have an important role to perform for my rudzwi.* He heard a hissing sound in his ear and he smiled. "Yes, my uncle I hear you; the snake man will be found and the rudzwi will have peace again."

Chapter 15

The morning was always the worst, Abigail thought as she lay in her bed. Her small body was pushed up against one side of the bed, as if she didn't deserve all this luxury and space. It felt right to keep herself small; in bed she was curled up, when walking she was hunched over, and when she sat she bunched up her legs so her frame was tight and unobtrusive. Some of her was aware she was trying to be small, invisible so she could be ignored and it would be OK. Her heart knew it wasn't OK. Her heart ached for her mother's affection and attention. Even her father seemed to have given up on her. He had always understood her, had seen through her and reached through when she pretended she didn't want anything. Not now; now he arrived home like a headless chicken, moving frenetically from one thing to the other, seemingly unable to stop and be still for a moment.

She heard her parents argue a lot these days. That hurt too, and she concluded it must be her fault. They snapped at each other; and at the dinner table she realized one day that they didn't look each other in the eyes when they talked. Their eyes skirted around each other's faces, staring at the cheeks or the neck. *Isn't that strange?* she thought. *Is that because of me, too?* and that was as far as she got. In fact when she studied it she saw that the whole family did that: no one really looked at each other's eyes. She would test it; she would look up and ask for the saltcellar, boring her eyes into her father as she did it. Quickly he avoided her gaze, pretending that he needed to see what was on his fork before he put it into his mouth.

She was desperate for friends, too, but Madeline had told so many stories about her that there was no chance of that. Other kids looked at her as if she were weird, as if she couldn't be trusted. When she asked for something they made out that they didn't hear, and moved away from her quickly.

She was tired of the pain. If she had s-something, the name in her mother's purse, then clearly this is what her life would be from now on. Lonely, so lonely it felt like she was going to break inside from the loneliness. She was convinced that the loneliness was devouring her heart, nibbling away at her softness, leaving distrust and bitterness in its wake. She also felt like her insides were made of thin glass, and they were all going to shatter one day, there was going to be a big explosion. What would happen then? She didn't know; maybe there would be such a big burst that all the dung beetle balls would torpedo out of her brain like missiles. That would be a good thing, surely, she responded to herself, folding into her body more and pulling the sheet over her head.

"Abigail, get up for school; you're late," she heard her mother say, irritation barely concealed in her voice. "I'm leaving, so your father will have to take you," she caught as her mother's voice started to fade.

"Abigail, I'm late for the office. You need to be dressed in five minutes; otherwise you'll have to take your bike to school," her father shouted impatiently.

"I'll go on my bike, Dad," she responded, sighing. She reached out her arm and put her pillow over her head trying to drown out the thoughts inside: *No one cares about you, Abigail, not even your mother and father. Your brother and sister don't play with you, you have no friends, and your sickness makes you a burden.* The same thoughts returned over and over again; the hurt was building on the hurt and merging with the loneliness. *Not even Zukah would like you now, nor Josef. You are never going to have a friend again.*

She was tired of these messages, the same tape playing over the dung beetle balls; it couldn't be erased. Her brain was no longer hers; she couldn't think other thoughts even though she tried. In the last month since her birthday, she'd heard, very softly at first and then louder, *You would be better off dead.* She tried not to listen to the voice. When that voice spoke, the smoke went crazy, spinning circles around her as if to give her strength. The smoke was her only friend now, she reflected. The smoke didn't ignore her, get irritated with her, pretend she wasn't there. It didn't treat her like a weirdo, shout at her, attack her with glaring eyes. The smoke accepted her. *It's hard to say if it loves me because it's smoke, but maybe it does.* She could especially believe that when she saw it swirling madly to protect her from dark thoughts like running into a car.

It felt like ages before she got up, and she knew it was too late to go to school. *What will I do today? I have no one to play with.* She responded internally, *I don't want to do anything.* The one helper the family had was on holiday; and her mother didn't come home until mid-afternoon. Abigail's thoughts started to darken: *Maybe I should take some pills,* she thought, *and maybe I can go to sleep for a couple of months, then wake up to a different life.*

Which pills? Well, there was the medicine cabinet; it had lots of pills. It was too dark inside to see the smoke. She could go outside and see what the smoke thought of that idea. *No, I won't; it will just be another dung beetle ball if the smoke does react.* Abigail knew her thoughts were dangerous, but she felt out of control; the loneliness was in charge of her life and it was impossible to fight back.

No one really cared anyway, of course everyone would be shocked but soon they would get over it. While she was in hospital, asleep for some time, they wouldn't have to worry each day about what was wrong with Abigail. *I'm tired of being a problem for everyone. It might help the family if I take the pills; there'll be one less problem.* Her father had enough problems at work, and Mom was so unhappy with her, it might help her to focus on herself. Darkness was building on darkness; the tunnel started to get smaller and smaller, and Abigail felt that she was in too deep now to escape. It felt like she had lost all control.

Abigail's heart started to beat loudly. The closer she got to the cabinet the stronger she could hear it. She reached up and grabbed the first pill bottle. She turned it around in her hands, feeling the clamminess of her hands as she fondled the bottle. It frightened her to see how her hands were reacting; they seemed to know how serious things were. She stared at the bottle, trying to read the label and decide how many she would need to put her to sleep for a couple of months. She didn't want to sleep forever, and she didn't want to die, but she wanted a different life when she woke up. She wanted things to be very different. How many should she take for that to happen? What if she took too many and died, what would happen to the family then? A flash of her mother's tormented face appeared like a shadow in front of her. Abigail felt her body shiver with fear. She looked down at her hand on the bottle; it was shaking, shaking with fear and desperation. Then inside she felt a shutter come down and she felt numb. *It will be the best for the family if they have a couple of months' break from me. Yes, it'll work for me and will help them too. Then when I come back, I'll start a new life. Things will be different and I won't have to be so lonely every day. Maybe when I come back I can see Zukah again; maybe when I come back I'll have some friends and I won't be such a burden to my family.*

She screwed open the lid of the pill bottle, not bothering to read the label because she concluded it would only confuse her. She felt reassured by her mind that it was the best thing; she felt certain now. She put all the pills in the bottle in her one hand, cupping it so they would not fall on the bathroom floor. When she looked at them, they seemed to stare at her, as if each pill had a set of eyes and they were all glaring at her. *How many?* Abigail placed the pill bottle on the back of the washroom basin and started to count the pills in her hand. She counted twenty-four. *How many?* she kept hearing in her mind. *If I take them all maybe I'll die,* she surmised, shivering again at the thought, but her decision felt cold and calculating now. A thought then popped into her mind: *Abigail don't do it, don't do it Abigail, we all love you.*

It's too late, thought Abigail in response; this was just the dung beetle balls trying to confuse her when she had made a decision. *Twelve, that's the right number to sleep for two or so months.* Quickly now she put some of the pills back in the bottle, counting what was remaining in her hand. She counted thirteen, hurriedly she put one back and ran to the kitchen to get a glass of water. She picked up the first glass she saw in the sink and turned the tap on; everything was suddenly urgent. She sensed if she didn't act quickly she would back out and the dung beetle balls would take over. Her hand started to shake again but she ignored it. She concentrated on opening her mouth as wide as she could, so her cupped hand was able to maneuver all the pills into her mouth. She reached over for the glass, tipping it so enough water was able to slide in after them. She started to swallow. Some pills had gone down but there were some trapped in her cheeks. Her body shuddered at the taste; they had started to melt and acidic foam was released around her back teeth. She swallowed more water, swirled it around, trying to catch all of the foam. Her mouth started to clear.

Suddenly fear kicked in, and urgent questions exploded in her psyche: *What have I done, what will happen to me, what if I die?* Abigail ran to the phone, her mind panicked, and at first she couldn't remember her mother's work number. Then in a flash it popped into her mind; frantically she pressed the numbers. Her head was starting to feel drowsy in spite of the panic. She heard her mother's voice, but it seemed like her mother was in a fog and was a long, long way away. Her voice was like someone else's voice.

"Mom, please help me, I took some pills, I wanted to go tooo ......" she heard her voice trail off, then heard a click on the phone. Some time later she felt her body crumple beneath her; she faintly heard a chair crash and felt a sharp blow to her head.

When Abigail started to wake, she could see shapes all around her. The shapes looked like they were coming closer and then disappearing. Her eyes tried to figure out the shapes but they were blurred. She then heard her mother's voice. The sounds were soothing, but she couldn't make contact with them, as if her mother were speaking a different language. Then she heard her father's voice; it was also full of softness, but her mind couldn't decipher the words. She fell asleep again.

Her parents sat on either side of the bed. Bill placed his hand on Jackie's, covering it and then making stroking motions along its side. He watched as tears flowed down her face, tears of torment, guilt, worry, tears of overwhelming love and confusion. Her head shook from side to side as if she couldn't take it all in. He didn't want to look into her eyes. He could just imagine the pain reflected in them as she stared down at her daughter's huddled form, helpless to help her as she battled through the effects of her overdose. He imagined she was thinking what he was thinking: Would Abigail's body come out of this unscathed? The doctor had reassured them that she was stable now, but he couldn't give any guarantees regarding long-term side effects. He murmured his response: "At this stage we just don't know. We'll have to wait until it clears her system."

Jackie had interjected in an anguished voice, "Will her brain be damaged?" The doctor had just shaken his head and repeated that he "just didn't know." Bill saw Jackie's body contort with the pain of it all. Her shoulders crumpled onto her chest and her head hung over her neck. He was scared to acknowledge her pain fully. It was overwhelming enough seeing his darling Abigail breathing heavily in front of him, her brow knotted in tension on her forehead, and a large grey smudge of a bruise protruding angrily on her left temple.

Bill noticed Jackie's head leaning a little closer, as if trying to will Abigail more strength. He could just imagine the self-recriminating thoughts she was having; he was having the same. He kept hearing them in his head: *You let your daughter down. She needed you and you weren't there. You got tired of all the conversations about smoke. You were too busy with work and politics to pay attention to her. You would have seen the build-up if you'd made the time for her.* He felt angry with himself; his sweet vulnerable family philosopher had been crying out for help and he had ignored the signs. Work had completely taken over, he realized now, given all that had been happening and the program for the returning refugees.

How could he have gotten so consumed that he had ignored his daughter's needs, been oblivious to her overwhelming distress? He felt sick and inadequate as a father and a husband. He could see that both his wife and daughter were suffering; but at the time there hadn't seemed to be anything he could do to make the pain go away. He had felt as if the family's pain were swallowing him up, as if he were diving into a well of pain and there were a chance he wouldn't be able to get out. It had felt like survival at the time, but survival for whom? His own survival, but at what cost to the family, the people he loved, his children and wife, the ones who gave his life meaning?

He knew a crisis had the ability to shine strobe lighting on past actions, and now he could see clearly that he had felt inadequate with the problems at work, too. His boss had started to drink heavily to deal with the stress of negotiating with the new government. It had unnerved him; he knew he would get tarred with the same brush if his boss got out of control. Bill knew from past experiences that as Jack drank more his anger would become less manageable. This government had a different flavor from the previous biracial government. There was an underlying animosity, understandably, thought Bill; but he prayed it would not lead to civil war. *With all this country has been through, it needs peace, as desperately as a skinny dog needs a crust of bread.*

He felt sick at the memory of the recent refugee debacle. He had followed departmental policy by insisting that any money sent for rations for the returning refugees must be accounted for, but the man in charge of the one refugee camp had been determined to flout the rules, acting nonplussed when asked for invoices, and then insisting that meat be included in the rations, which would have raised the cost astronomically. Bill recalled his exasperation as he'd implored the man for invoices and accounting. He'd managed to secure funding from Sweden, the U.S, Holland, Germany and France, but the funds had not all come through and the money was running out. Of course he had to challenge the camp leader when two weeks of rations disappeared in five days, and there were no invoices. He'd heard reports that people at some camps were selling the government handouts at a profit. He knew some Africans in charge of the camps saw him as an obstructionist, but he had to hold the line and risk unpopularity to do the right thing.

Bill went over it again, recalling when Jack reported that the rebellious camp leader had complained to the Minister. The camp leader had accused him of deliberately using red tape to block the refugees' access to supplies; the accusation carried an implication of racism. Apparently it had been reported in Parliament. The claim sickened him. He knew the camp leader had been angry with him, but he was shocked to learn of the complaint. Surely his reputation would stand him in good stead; surely the Africans knew he had been on their side all this time. Surely his past actions and integrity would protect him at this time of great volatility. Something gnawed inside, and he felt less secure, as if his foundation were made of poorly set jelly.

Now looking down at his struggling daughter, he remonstrated himself for getting so embroiled in work when his own child was in such need. Just then Abigail yawned and opened her eyes for a moment before going back to sleep. His heart leaped; maybe she was going to be all right after all. He felt a wave of relief followed by a river of worry: Would she have brain damage? Had she damaged some organs? Would it be his fault? He could have helped her before she got so desperate. He knew she was lonely; he knew her school friends had rejected her; he knew she felt alone with her experience with the smoke; he knew she thought that the world around her was judging her. A flash of her taking the pills took over his mind: He saw her small hand go up to her mouth with the pills in her hand, and anger rose in him like lava about to spew. He held his breath pushing it down, compartmentalizing it, cutting himself off from it.

He felt angry, too, with Jackie for assuming their daughter was schizophrenic right from the start. He sensed that Abigail had internalized Jackie's fear of that illness. But now was not the time to let his anger out at Jackie.

His baby girl, she had been through so much on her own. How could he ever forgive himself? How would Jackie handle this? She had already been depressed and depleted even before Abigail's overdose. There was a lot of work ahead of them, but he committed to put every ounce of effort he could into helping his daughter restore and find herself again.

If only he could have assurance she was going to be OK. It would be all right, as long as she didn't suffer long-term consequences for this. It would kill him if his daughter became disabled in some way because of his neglect. If she had been born that way, he would have accepted it; but to have scarred his child by neglectful parenting would be hell on earth for him, and surely for Jackie, too, every hour, day and month a reminder of their failure as parents. A jail term would be easier to handle than that purgatory. He looked at his watch; how long had they been there? He'd rushed to the hospital the moment Jackie had sobbed into the phone at around ten thirty in the morning. It was now ten past seven. He hadn't eaten all day; at the realization, he became suddenly aware of a voracious hunger. Thank goodness Jackie had called Martha, their closest friend, and arranged for her to stay the night with Samantha and Stephen.

"Would you like a sandwich, Jackie?" he whispered, careful to keep his voice as soothing as possible in case Abigail heard it.

"I'm not hungry, Bill but you go right ahead; I'll stay." She shook her head as she stared at her daughter's mass of hair and small face, swallowed in amongst the starched white pillows and white sheets.

Bill felt the weight of Jackie's pain. *Abigail has to come through unscathed,* he thought again. Jackie would not be able to cope. He couldn't think of the consequences for the family anymore. It was all too overwhelming. Right now, he had to think positively so his daughter could draw on his strength. *She'll be all right—she'll come through this,* he affirmed. Then as a family we would take note of everything that had contributed to the nightmare Abigail had been living. *I have to change. I have to live a life that reflects my love of my wife and family.* Then one last affirmation: *We will get through.*

He noticed he felt a little lighter as he handed over the money to the African woman selling sandwiches in the small hospital cafeteria. The cafeteria looked a little run down *Who cares?* he thought. *This is hardly the time to do an assessment of how the government is managing health care. Nothing matters as long as my daughter is going to be OK.* Where had getting caught up in politics gotten him, anyway? He'd been boiling in a stew of daily discontent while the country undertook a massive transition. He cared deeply for the country and its people, but his role was bound to keep diminishing. Developments were out of his hands, like so much of his life. *Everything I can control is right here, with my family. This is where I need to put my energy.* He wanted desperately to feel close to Jackie and the kids again.

Jackie looked up as soon as he walked back into the room, her face awash with peace and her eyes aglow with a light Bill hadn't seen on her face in what felt like years. "Bill, she mentioned Zukah twice since you left: she rolled over softly, said 'Zukah,' and then after that she called for Robin and then fell back asleep. Her brain can't be badly damaged, Bill, not if she remembers their names." She started to sob, silently at first, then her whole body was heaving and she gave in to her relief as she bent over Abigail's crumpled form in the bed.

Bill, crying now too, squeezed next to his wife and put his arm around her. He felt her fold into his body like an acrobat falling into the net. He stroked her arm; he had gotten his wife back, and his tears, too, were of relief. Jackie looked up at his eyes and wiped his tears with tender fingertips. He felt the intense intimacy of the moment and pulled her back to him. "We're going to be all right, Jackie; we're going to get through this and our baby will be fine," he whispered tenderly in her ear. He felt her arms hugging him, drawing him closer, a hug that reminded him of their early dating days. Her eyes looked deeply into his, he felt the spark of the old connection between their souls; he couldn't remember how long it had been since she'd stared into his eyes. He felt his heart softening, letting her in again as he stared at her sparkly blue eyes through their glaze of tears. *I have my Jackie back,* he said to himself, *and my baby is going to be OK. We'll get stronger than ever before.* Eventually they collapsed on the end of the bed together.

Bill woke up disoriented in the middle of the night. His back was sore; he must have been sleeping in a strange position. He sat up and realized they were in the hospital; he and Jackie had been sleeping at the foot of Abigail's bed. Quickly he looked over to Abigail and tried to make out her form in the half-dimmed artificial twilight that was as close as the hospital got to darkness. She was breathing deeply, and so was Jackie. He lay back on the bed and tried to get comfortable again. The bed was big but still only a small space existed where he would not lie on either Jackie or Abigail. He curled into that space and, soothed by the renewed sense of closeness to his wife and the assurance that his daughter would be all right, he drifted back to sleep.

It was only in the late morning that Abigail's body started to get restless; and eventually her eyes opened. Jackie and Bill had sat in a daze on the end of the bed for hours, waiting desperately for that moment. Every now and then they had clutched each other's hands, squeezing tightly for a sense of security. Abigail had called out "Zukah!" and "Aunt Robin!" a number of times; each time Bill's sense of relief deepened. He wondered, though, how it could be that his daughter had grown so out of touch with the world that she only felt safe with a dead aunt and the son of a neighbor's former gardener, neither of whom she had ever seen more than sporadically. *Why not with me? Have I really been so absent?* It was hard to piece it all together. Sure, the politics of the country had been overwhelming, especially the returning refugees but how could he have been so absent as a parent?

Bill started to think again about the issue of signing checks. He had called the Minister as soon as Jack told him there had been a complaint about him being obstructionist with bureaucratic details. The Minister had commented with calculated casualness, "Maybe you'd be better-suited to another Ministry," an implied threat to his job. Bill had completely blocked out his memory of that detail, and shuddered as it came back to him. As soon as he had opened his mouth he'd felt branded, lumped in with the other racist whites, one of many not to be trusted. He had tried to explain why his actions were a sign of good governance; but the more he spoke the more he felt himself falling into a cavernous hole. The Minister had responded, "I will have to report to my boss that you are not willing to sign the checks for our freedom fighters." His tone had sounded ominous and threatening.

Bill had replied frantically, "Minister, I'm willing, but I cannot sign a blank check. All government departments need to account for their expenditures. I can't sign away money when we have no record of how it's being spent. Our funding is tight; some of the international funders like the United States haven't followed through with their promises yet."

From the moment the Minister had simply repeated his statement, Bill had realized that, in spite of decades of working closely with the Africans, forming close friendships, and priding himself on his cross-cultural sensitivity, his career was now on the line. What would happen, and what would he do? He had to have a job. It was so important to him to contribute to the transition. He had always been supportive of a black government; surely everyone knew that. When he'd felt control slipping away from him, his response had been to work harder. For about the last year he had started to come home later; at first it was once a week, but lately it had crept up to three or four nights a week. He would creep into the house after the whole family was in bed, then wake up the next morning and rush to the office. No wonder his daughter experienced him as absent; he had gone AWOL. No wonder Jackie had felt abandoned; in their time of need, where had he been? At the office, frantically pushing papers as he tried to strike up bonds with those he needed to work with in the future. He had put his own daughter at risk. If he had waited to drive her to school that morning, her overdose wouldn't have happened, might never have happened. The image of his daughter throwing pills into her mouth as a final act of desperation flashed up again. He held his breath for some time, pushing down against the angry turbulence that arose within him. His daughter felt closer to her dead aunt than to her living father—that really was shocking. Today, he resolved, was the first day in a whole new life, a life in which family would come first. If he lost his job, well, he would survive somehow. However, if he lost his family, he knew he would be a broken man, likely for the rest of his life.

Abigail opened her eyes again; this time she kept them open. He could feel Jackie trembling next to him; he reached over and squeezed her hand again to soothe her, calm her so they could be strong for their daughter.

"Where am I?" Abigail croaked. Just as she said it, a flash went through her mind of the pills, the acidic foam in her mouth, her hand trembling. She looked up, feeling sheepish, embarrassed, and guilty in front of her parents. She felt small, as if she had somehow regressed to a younger age. Were they going to be angry? She'd wanted to wake up to a different life, but what would that life be like?

"You're in hospital, Abigail," her mother responded in a loving voice, her eyes taking Abigail in. "I'm so glad you're awake and talking, darling."

"I'm sorry," Abigail said, starting to cry. Her head dropped back on the pillow, and the tears flowed out of her like a stream that had waited for years to be released. She pulled her hair over her face to cover up her shame, her hurt and the overwhelming guilt.

She felt a hand on her head stroking her hair, and another hand squeezing her hand. She heard her father say softly, "Sweetie, it's going to be all right. We're all in this together. I'm sorry, sweetie, I'm sorry I wasn't there for you."

At first Abigail was too consumed to take in her parents' words. Her pain was so strong that she felt she would die from it right there. It felt as if she were releasing all the loneliness, the dung beetle balls, the rejections and the hurt all at once. She felt her body rock in the bed, as if her chest were going to burst open with all the intense experiences that had been trapped for so long. She curled up in a fetal position and continued to sob; she wondered if she would ever stop. She felt someone's arms around her and another hand stroking her back. It felt soothing. She couldn't remember being touched like this; maybe she had, but it had been so long. Eventually the crying stopped, but the back rub and the firm hug continued.

Abigail moved her body and started to sit up, only to have a nurse run over to her bed and prop her up with pillows supporting her. "If you feel dizzy," the nurse said in a quiet voice, "then lie back down." She was a young woman. Her hair was tied back in a ponytail, and her blue, inquisitive eyes contrasted with her stiff white uniform.

"How are you feeling sweetie?" her mother ventured, sounding eager to strike a connection with her, to reassure her that things would change.

"I'm OK," said Abigail, still sheepishly trying still to hide behind her mass of tousled hair, her eyes furtively poking through.

"We understand why you were unhappy, Abigail," her mother reassured in a strong and loving tone. "Your father and I understand why you got so desperate. We're sorry we didn't realize sooner. We want to help in any way we can. You know we love you, sweetie."

Abigail didn't know what to say. She hadn't heard her mother speak like this for years; she was with her, not drifting off somewhere else. She noticed her parents were holding hands; this was strange too. Was this really the same family? Had someone cast a magic spell, had the smoke somehow transformed her life?

Bill reiterated, "You know how much we love you, Abigail. I'm sorry I was so busy at work that I didn't notice how much you were suffering. I promise you, Abigail, I won't do that again. My family is my priority, but please promise you'll never do anything like this again. Your mother and I need that promise."

Abigail pushed her hair over her face; it felt like there was a dung beetle ball in her mouth, she felt incapable of conversation. She stared at the bedding, ignoring her parents' intense gaze, feeling awkward with all the attention. It had been so long since she had gotten this kind of attention. Aunt Robin had given her total attention all of the time; also Zukah and Josef, but her parents had been otherwise engaged for years, it seemed, or maybe it was only months; for whatever reason it had seemed like forever.

"Yes, I promise. I'm sorry. I'll be OK," she said at last, "but I have to see Zukah, can you take me to Zukah?" she inquired emphatically, feeling her head clear more as she said it.

"Whatever would help you, sweetie; I'll take you to Umtali to see Zukah," Dad responded enthusiastically, as if relieved he could do something concrete to show his daughter that things had changed.

Her mother followed up quickly, "Is there anything else that would help you, darling? Anything at all I can do?" Abigail heard a faint emphasis on the "I," as if her mother felt left out.

"Stop seeing me as one of your patients," Abigail blurted out, "and assuming that I have that S disease. I know I was bad to take the pills, I didn't want to die, I wanted a new life."

Jackie felt punched in the stomach. Abigail was right; she had looked on her daughter like a patient. But how could she not, with all her talk about smoke and voices, and now taking a bottle of pills. *I didn't factor that into the equation; I should have done a suicide assessment.* However, she realized now that instead of loving her daughter and staying close to her, she had spent a good deal of time assessing her clinically. Her focus had been on looking for new symptoms and making judgments about her "patient's" mental health. It must have increased her daughter's loneliness, she surmised, undermining their relationship and putting distance between them. Guilt and shame showered over Jackie. She'd done everything with the best of intentions, but it had alienated her from her daughter at a time when she needed her the most. She'd been a mental health worker at home. How come she hadn't figured that out? She felt ashamed of herself, ashamed that her fear had become so compelling.

"I'm sorry, Abigail, I don't know what else to say, but I'm sorry."

Chapter 16

The family sat down at the oval dinner table, taking their usual places. Abigail noticed her mother sitting stiffly in her chair, and her father was perched off the edge of his seat. The lemon-bright color of the tablecloth offset the dark tension she sensed in her parents. Abigail squirmed in her chair. Her mother coughed a number of times; Abigail knew from past experience that was never a good sign. She felt her heart's pace quicken.

"Your father and I have been chatting," Mom blurted, coughing repeatedly after the statement. Jackie picked up each plate and laid some steaming trout on each one. All eyes focused on her. When Samantha pushed her hair out of her eyes, Abigail noticed a flash of worry through the steam of the carrots and parsnips.

"Yes, we've been chatting." Mom cleared her throat nervously. "Robin's will was sent to us some time ago; she's left us a small house that she owned before she met her husband. It's in Vancouver, Canada; it's a really beautiful city. We hadn't told you yet, but the Minister demanded that Dad hand in his resignation for his job, saying he wasn't the right person for the new government. Dad is currently training the new person who will take over his position." She coughed again, veering her mouth away from the fish below.

Bill quickly interjected, "Yes, and I recently applied for a job with the Canadian government. I got a call last week and they've offered it to me. It's in Vancouver, so we'll be emigrating as soon as we sell the house."

"Vancouver!" shouted Stephen. "I don't even know where that is. Why did the Minister ask you to leave, Dad?"

Bill, still reeling in shock at having been fired, tried to respond firmly; he had to be strong in the face of his family's distress. "It's a long story, Stephen, but the Minister felt the department would be more efficient without me there. I'm saddened by it, but there's nothing I can do. Your mother and I decided it's a good time to leave; we love the country, but it'll be difficult for me to get a new job here given the political climate. Vancouver is on the West coast of Canada. Remember, your aunt Robin used to speak of Vancouver, don't you remember Stephen?"

"She never spoke to me of Vancouver," Stephen grumbled. "Anyway, what will happen to my school, and what about my rugby? They probably don't play rugby over there."

"There are some good schools near the house that Robin has left us; she bought the house with my mother's money, so it's an important family inheritance. We'll look into rugby for you once we're there."

"I don't want to leave Zimbabwe," Abigail shouted, ratcheting up the tension. "I don't want to leave! What about Zukah?"

"Don't shout, Abigail," Bill replied. "You'll see Zukah tomorrow, and we'll come back to Zimbabwe every year, I promise. Every year we'll make sure you see Zukah." Bill spoke forcefully but with compassion.

He didn't want to tell the children that the chances of him finding employment again in the department were nil. He hadn't told them about the day that he was threatened with jail if he didn't sign the blank checks for the returning combatants. He had stood his ground, but his reputation was in the gutter from that day on, and his new African boss began ignoring him.

He hadn't mentioned a word of his previous white boss getting fired, nor of Jack's rampage through the department that led to the police hauling him away for a week. He wanted to shield them from all of it; he wanted them to feel safe in spite of the political earthquakes all around them. He didn't want them to join the other white children whose racist mutterings slipped off their tongues with ease. He knew the family could not live on Jackie's salary; and who knew how long her job was guaranteed. The family needed to make a change now if they were to have a secure future. He didn't want to go into that with the children; it would increase their insecurity. Jackie and he had discussed at length how to put it across. He had expected the first disclosure to be the worst, but still they had a lot to get through. He understood how disruptive it would be to all of their lives; but with his career in jeopardy it really was the only way forward. The family needed more stability in their future. The thought of leaving the country pained him, but he would have to put aside his own feelings for the sake of the family.

"I don't like the cold," Samantha sneaked out, "and my best friend, what about her?"

"Just as Abigail will see Zukah once a year, we will make sure you will see Jane. I know it's hard, Samantha, but we don't know what will happen in Zimbabwe in the future. If we're going to move, the time is now, while I can still get employment. As your Mom and I get older, it gets harder for us to find jobs."

"What about all the birds, the frogs and the wild animals? I'll miss them," Abigail responded angrily.

Jackie began, "You heard what Dad said, Abigail; we'll visit once a ..."

"But I love Africa, I love it here, I don't want to go to the cold like Samantha, why do we have to g..."

"That's enough, Abigail," Bill asserted. "Stephen and Samantha, I can see you're also not happy, but the decision has been made, so let's eat supper in silence and we can discuss it again tomorrow. Case closed."

The children knew when their father was this forceful it was not the time to talk. Slowly Abigail picked away at the fish and vegetables on her plate. Finally she mumbled, "I'm not hungry" and excused herself from the table. She expressed her unhappiness by scraping her chair on the hardwood floor, then moved away abruptly. She wondered what the smoke would have to say about this move to Canada. Would the smoke follow her there or not? Would she be leaving the smoke behind? How would she manage? Life had started feeling a bit better, but would she fall back into the loneliness in Canada? How would she able to say goodbye to Zukah tomorrow, knowing she wouldn't see him for a year?

Abigail sat on her bed and listened as her questions emerged. She wanted the smoke's response to this news, before she got totally depressed and angry. She clutched her pillow and sat on her bed cross-legged and completely still, and waited for a response to drop in.

"*Canada will be good for your heart,*" reassured the voice. "*It will grow there. Zukah will always be with you. Remember, wherever you go, the smoke goes.*"

Abigail released the pillow and just stared, stunned at the ease with which the voice came in, almost like a phone call. *The smoke says the move will be a good thing.* Soon after the relief, however, doubt set in again. *Maybe I'm just making it all up. I still need Zukah to explain about the smoke and whether I've gone mad or whether I do really have the S disease.* She clasped her hands together in prayer: *Please, Zukah, help me tomorrow. Help me understand about the smoke, and what's happened to me and whether I'll cope in Canada.*

Abigail had wondered if this morning would ever come. She couldn't remember when she started counting the number of sleeps until she could see Zukah. Finally the day had arrived, and the birds seemed to let her know that today was an important day. A robin had perched on her windowsill and sung as if its heart were about to burst. Today was even more important now that the family were leaving. She had woken up several times in the night, terrified that her life would become a mess again if she left the country and Zukah. She remembered the day when her father had flown into the lounge while the family watched a nature show on TV. He had announced loudly that he had finally made contact with Josef through the neighbor's gardener's friend, and Josef had said they were welcome for a visit. When her father told her the news, Abigail thought her heart would get attacked with excitement. Finally, after months since her stay in hospital, she would see Zukah, sweet sweet Zukah, who understood her, who thought about things she did, who really knew her. He would understand the smoke and the voices in her head; he would have an explanation. She was convinced of it.

Since the day of taking the pills she had been talking more openly and so had her parents. Samantha and Stephen were also treating her differently since her hospital stay. She felt she received more respect from them, as if they really did care. Samantha included her in games she played with her friends, and she had started to get on really well with her one friend Julia. She still felt guilty about her overdose; occasionally she would have a flash of her parents' faces at her bedside. Their eyes had looked as if they'd retreated to the cavernous pits of hell. She had never seen them look so sick with worry, and this was worry she had caused. She noticed once they'd started talking with her that the shroud had lifted a bit. She knew they had always loved her, but they had become shadowy figures in her life, so removed from her reality that she couldn't count on them anymore. She remembered that the loneliness had been unbearable, but these days it was hard to imagine it.

Her mother seemed a bit more alive now, and she wasn't questioning her as much. She would ask sometimes about the smoke and voices but Abigail didn't feel like her patient undergoing assessment. She no longer felt invisible in her parents' company. Her father was spending more time at home. Gone were those late evenings when they would hear his car coming up the driveway stealthily, like a furtive creature trying not to be noticed. The family all had supper together now, and the conversations were like the old times. Stephen and Samantha were still arguing; but even their arguments seemed friendlier, as if underneath it all they still liked each other. There were lots of discussions and heated conversations that she liked. She liked hearing different ideas and feeling the passion flowing. Yes, the family was alive again.

She wondered if this would all change again if they went to Canada. Vancouver was on her mind, but she pushed it to the back. *Today is the day I see Zukah. I have a lot to tell him, so I'll think about that.* She would tell Zukah about the smoke and the role that it played in her life. Talking to others who had no understanding of the smoke and its voice seemed pointless now. *They don't know what to say so there's no use,* she concluded. *Zukah has understood everything else about me, like Aunt Robin did, before she died. As long as one person understands I'll be all right.* When her mother had asked about the smoke in a more curious way recently, Abigail had just said that it didn't bother her anymore. She could see the relief on her mother's face; Mom must have assumed that because Abigail had said it didn't bother her, somehow it had gone away. That was fine for now, Abigail thought; bringing it up would only worry Mom again. Holding on for Zukah was the best thing she could do; the voices in her head said the same.

"Are you ready, Abigail?" she heard her father shout from outside.

"Yes, Dad, I'm coming."

She quickly picked up her bag and checked again that her present for Zukah was in there. Abigail took one last look at herself in the mirror before she hurried outside. Her face looked lighter, brighter, as if someone had come in the night and scrubbed her. The confusion too was feeling more manageable these days, as if the big dung beetle balls had melted. It was a normal load of confusion, and the confusion was living in a smaller part of her brain. It was now easier to think, to have conversations, to know what she felt. Maybe the pills had washed the bad stuff away. Whatever had happened, she thought as she rushed through the passage on her way to the car, she felt grateful.

The whole family stood by the car, waiting to see her off. Samantha had a small brown bag in her hand and was swinging it up and down. Her hair was pulled back and her eyes were more visible than usual. "I made you some cookies to give to Zukah," she said shyly walking over to Abigail.

Abigail started to tear up; feeling embarrassed by the attention. "Thanks, Sam," she mumbled reaching over to touch her shoulder. Abigail looked at her mother and brother; she saw their excited faces. both beaming, even though it was early on a Saturday morning and they hadn't had breakfast yet.

"Thanks, everyone, thanks," she said self-consciously, pulling her hair over her face to hide her reaction. She pulled open the car door, then quickly nestled into the seat and wound down the window. "C'mon Dad, or we'll be late," she bellowed, now taking charge of the moment.

"OK, Abigail, let's go," Bill responded, feeling as excited as the rest of the family. He knew this was a critical step in the family's healing.

After some time on the journey African villagers were starting to appear on the side of the road. Bill knew the route to Umtali; he had travelled there frequently for work. He remarked to himself how everything had changed since they had turned onto the dirt road, as if they had entered another country. The pace had changed dramatically. Dogs languished in the road, as if they knew instinctively they could laze about without losing their lives to barreling metal cages. Potholes forced cars to move slowly, meandering to one side and then the next like a river unsure of its direction. Red dust followed their car like a shadow; it swirled and then descended, hovering over the car in a red cloak that grew thicker as the journey progressed. Nature was in charge here, thought Bill, as he circumvented a deep crevice in the road, narrowly missing a goat that had escaped through a fence. He could hear the squeals of the African children behind them, heard their piercing laughter echo as they retrieved the goat. What a contrast, he thought, between this world and the "white world" he inhabited. The rhythms were like those of the earth, slow, mellifluous, and unfolding, not the scattered, headless-chicken pace he had gotten caught up in before Abigail's hospitalization. He stopped the car to wait for a man to drag his cow across to the other side. The man's black face beamed through the red haze; he slowly made his way across. Bill felt he was watching a deliciously slow-paced movie. *It's a good reminder to live slowly. Before we leave, I must bring the kids out to the Domboshawa area; it's just like this.*

"Are we nearly there, Dad?" Abigail piped, sitting up erect and straining to see further than the road just ahead.

"Another ten minutes, sweetie. We're on time; Josef and Zukah are expecting us at eleven."

"I'm sure Zukah and Josef don't have a watch, Dad. That's the way we live, but they don't live that way." She swung her head from side to side, expressing her mild annoyance at her father's ignorance.

"I know, Abigail. I could learn a lot from their way of life," he said, guiltily still remembering his phase of excessive work when he felt numb and robotic, and was oblivious to his daughter's plight.

Abigail started to play with her hair, her fingers twirling it more frantical-ly as the time passed. Today was an important day. She knew she had been able to keep her spirits up and feel calmer because she instinctively felt Zukah would have some answers for her. But what if he didn't, what if he didn't believe her about the smoke and the voices, what if he treated her like Madeline did? Would her loneliness and confusion build again, would she get more dung beetle balls back in her brain, and then would everyone start treating her differently again? She knew if that happened the devastation would be unbearable. She had made a pact with herself never to harm herself again, but she wanted to be happy, she wanted to feel understood, she wanted to feel normal. She liked having Julia as a friend now. Even Rick and some other girls were talking to her normally these days, as if they liked her. Since Madeline had gone to another school things had changed. It was a massive relief; yes, she wanted things to stay normal. It was scaring her now, now she was this close to speaking to Zukah. What if he said he didn't want to see her in a year's time? Maybe with her going to Canada he would say there was no point in meeting again. Who would she turn to then? It had been OK not to talk to her parents about the smoke and the voices anymore, because she had imagined Zukah giving her everything she needed. If he didn't, would she feel desperate again? How would she manage if he didn't understand? Sure, she felt clearer and lighter now but that could all change if Zukah rejected her.

Bill sensed the shift in her mood. He could see her body get tighter; whenever she crunched herself up in a ball as if trying to disappear; he knew she was having a tough time.

"What's up, Abigail?" he said gently, hoping not to get a defensive reaction.

"Oh, nothing," she mumbled, covering her mouth with her hair.

The familiar feeling of helplessness began to rise in him again, the helpless feeling that had driven him to seek crazy distraction in his work. Bill knew he had to handle this carefully. Instinctively, he knew it was vital that Abigail speak with Zukah. What if she backed out?

Would she retreat as she had before and throw him and the rest of the family back into a tailspin? *Take your time*, he coached himself. *Go slowly; she's scared for some reason.*

"I don't want to go, Dad. Please, turn around." Abigail sounded panicked, as if fear had taken control of her, filled her brain, kept her from thinking clearly.

What should he say? What would Jackie say if they returned without a meeting? Bill fought the heavy feeling of panic and tried to speak calmly, as if he had a real grip on the situation. "Sweetie" was all he could manage.

"Turn around, Dad, please turn around. I don't want to see Zukah; I've changed my mind. I'll wait until we come back from Canada for a visit." She could scarcely believe the words coming out of her mouth. She knew deep down that today's visit was exactly what she needed, but the risk was more than she could bear; it was as if some force had taken over her voice.

"Abigail, you know and I know ..." but Dad stopped, as if he'd forgotten what he was going to say. She could tell he was panicking with her, and it only made things worse to see the fear controlling him, too. She saw the smoke whirling in front of her eyes, moving from side to side as if it were angry and fighting with her. She tried to ignore it at first, but then she stared, magnetized by it. Then the voice came into her head: *"Abigail, you must meet Zukah."* That was all it said.

She knew she needed to talk about what she had experienced, about everything that had happened since Aunt Robin died. Maybe she should force herself to meet Zukah, even though she was scared. She had to talk to someone about her strange experiences before she left the country. If not Zukah, who? There was no one else with whom she could take the risk. Josef and Zukah were the only people she knew who might understand about the smoke and voices. Her desperation seemed to be clearing the fear a little bit. It was still there, but somehow she found more strength to manage it. She looked over and saw her father's face; he looked almost as distraught as when she'd awakened from the overdose. She felt guilty; she couldn't put her parents through that again. *He wants the best for me,* she reminded herself, *and he's doing this for me.* Allies were joining her side against the fear.

Silence sat heavy in the car. What would she say now? How could she respond? "OK Dad, I'm scared but I'll go," she blurted, not knowing if she had made the right decision, but relieved to have found the courage to give it a try.

Dad looked over with such relief and love on his face that she felt sheepish. "Good for you, Abigail, good for you," was all he said, but it was enough; his face said it all.

A couple of minutes later Bill pulled over to park under a tree. The sun was intense, even piercing the shady areas with its heat rays; he could feel the burning on his skin as he slammed the door shut. Josef had told him to take the path off the side road, after the big jacaranda that was past the school. The directions had all seemed a bit vague, but it was coming together now. He looked over in the distance and saw the familiar mud huts all nestled together; they formed a circle as if around some mystical force in the center. He had never been in one and was curious.

"C'mon, Abigail," he beckoned, seeing her small form in her pink shorts and blue t-shirt hesitating around the other side of the car.

She pushed her hair back, as if she had to prepare herself for the moment ahead by clearing her view so she could take it all in. She moved next to him, as if into the protection of a towering tree. Bill sensed her vulnerability and put his arm around her, squeezing her shoulder as if his hug could inject strength into her body. She seemed so frail and so strong at the same time; he felt he needed to protect her and yet could lean on her. Who did she take after? he reflected. She was philosophical like him, but overall more like his sister, he thought. Robin had the spirit of an intrepid world traveler, her courage almost bursting through her skin sometimes. He remembered her other side too, easily hurt, so sensitive and perceptive. Yes, Abigail was most like Robin, come to think of it. Neither he nor Jackie could match either of their wild sides.

As they moved onto the path Bill pushed her gently ahead of him, encouraging her to take the lead in their venture. She moved tentatively at first, her small feet kicking up the dust; hesitating every now and then. The closer they got to the mud huts the faster her stride became. She seemed to find renewed strength, and her feet fell with determination, stamping at the dusty path so it rose to greet her. They moved through a clearing and started to see African bodies in the distance. One was hunched over a wooden container and banging the contents with a large stick. They could hear the pounding, like a heartbeat: *boom, da boom, boom.* Bill could make out the shape of a woman. The cloths tied to her body danced around her with enough energy to make it seem that her clothing was as alive as she. He saw some children running around, chasing each other, and then chasing some chickens into an enclosed area.

Abigail shot her arm up into the air as soon as she saw Zukah. He was talking with an older man near the woman who was pounding the corn. When the boy saw her, he stopped and moved toward her. Abigail felt her heart leap. Excitement and trepidation mixed together and she felt charged by it all. Dad stayed behind, as if some instinct held him back.

Temba felt his legs moving quickly; as he got closer to Abigail and saw her form more clearly his heart pounded. His white sister, his African flower! Her presence, her companionship, his love for her was medicine for the anger he felt in a racialized world. Even though the government had changed, the anger had not left his heart, nor the confusion of why a black skin was inferior to a white skin. His white sister would help him. Just being close to her, like a brother to a sister, just feeling her acceptance would drain some of the dark feelings he still felt.

As soon as Abigail saw him, taller and more manly than she remembered, she felt her body relax with relief. She could surrender at last and be safe. She knew he would understand—she felt as soon as he was next to her that she didn't even have to explain herself anymore; somehow she just knew he would be able to help her. He hugged her; she didn't remember hugging him before but it felt right. She sensed they needed each other now more than before.

"Zukah, my father came to visit too," she said nervously, feeling awkward that her father was hovering over her.

"Aah, Mr. Bill, how are you?" He took the white man's hand and cupped it between his own in a friendly gesture.

Bill felt struck by the changes in Zukah since he had last seen him. He couldn't put his finger on it, but something was different. He looked closely at the boy's face. Zukah's lovely brown skin shone as if a light were coming through it; he radiated goodness and his senses seemed alive. His coffee-colored eyes sparkled as he looked at Abigail, and his face opened with a smile that revealed luminous teeth. Everything about him seemed bright. Bill hadn't noticed this in him before, and suddenly Bill was struck by the wisdom in the boy's face. Did this young boy have something to teach him? *He's able to be close to my daughter in spite of her circumstances; he is able to understand her in ways I find hard.* Bill felt open and grateful that the meeting had finally come together.

"You look different, Zukah," Bill told him, "like a young man going in the right direction. I can't put my finger on it, but you've grown somehow."

"Mr. Bill, many things have changed: my uncle died, I took on a new role in the village, and my name now is Temba." Temba looked down, honoring his uncle by claiming his name again in public.

"Temba," Abigail and Bill said together, and Bill continued, "I don't understand."

"It is strange for white culture, but in Shona society, when someone dies, a close relative can become a vessel for his spirit. I have become that vessel for my uncle." He spoke emphatically, expecting the white man to offer a dismissive rebuttal but ready to hold his ground.

Bill hesitated. He looked over to Abigail and noticed a grin forming on her face. How could he respond? He didn't have any experience of spirits. It wasn't that he thought the boy was lying, but without any knowledge, what could he say? "Uh, a vessel," he managed, feeling his ground shifting.

"Yes, a vessel," Temba reiterated, standing taller but feeling uncomfortable; they had already ventured into territory unknown to a white man and a black teenager in Zimbabwe.

"I'm not sure I understand," Bill admitted shuffling his feet back and forth. He looked over Temba's head and saw Josef slowly moving toward them. He felt relieved the conversation would soon be over; he didn't really know what to say. He knew from his Christian teaching that God came through people's minds and gave messages, but he didn't know about being a vessel for dead people; that seemed strange. He knew from speaking to his African friends that they had many beliefs that were different from his, and he enjoyed hearing about their culture, but no one had ever talked about spirits, dead people and vessels. Best he leave this topic alone.

"Boss Boyd, how are you Boss Boyd?" Josef said enthusiastically, smiling at Abigail at the same time. "We are pleased to see you and your young daughter." Josef stood tall, his body clothed in traditional cloths secured around his waist and an open shirt baring some of his black chest and hairs. Bill noticed sweat on his brow, and although his expression was warm and friendly there was also some hesitancy in the way he held his body back.

"Thank you for letting us visit. Abigail has had a tough time and we all felt Zukah, sorry Temba, would be comforting for her to talk to." Bill felt his body straighten and was pleased he was now on firmer ground.

"We are sorry to hear you have been suffering, Abigail. You are a strong spirit, and we are honored to be of help."

He's right, Bill thought; *she is a strong spirit.* He sensed the two Africans' compassion for his daughter, and he felt uplifted, certain now that Temba was going to be able to help.

"You are good people," he responded humbly, then added, *"Mazvita,"* thanking them in Shona.

Josef smiled, cupping his hands in gratitude. "Temba, take Abigail for a walk to the river. Go to the place where the river wakes up and we will join you later, after Boss Boyd and I have had some tea."

"Call me Bill, please, Josef."

"I will take her, father," Temba responded with excitement. "Abigail, come with me." *Her small body houses a big spirit,* he reflected; *she is young but her spirit is old. We have much in common, even if our skin color is different.*

Abigail followed as a sheep follows the shepherd. She was safe, safe after all this time, safe to say what she needed to say without trying to think how it would sound. She didn't have to worry now whether she would be judged or rejected, for in her heart she knew Zukah would respond in a way that would soothe her. *If only he hadn't gone away I wouldn't have suffered for this long. I wouldn't have taken all those pills. I wouldn't have put my family through hell.*

"Tell me again why you became Temba?" she asked, wanting to know everything about his life since she had seen him leaving on her way to school. It felt strange for her to see where he lived. She knew he lived in a village; she had seen many villages on the family hikes, but she had never visited a village like a guest. They walked along the bush-lined path. Occasionally there was an acacia tree with spearing thorns that hung over and provided soothing shade, but for the most part the path wove through the harsh midday sunlight, cooking their bodies below.

"My uncle Temba died," Temba related. "He was killed by a snake. That is why my father returned to be the village headman, to take over his place. The village was deeply troubled because we learned someone placed the snake in the field near where Temba was working. In the Shona tradition it is common for someone to be the vessel, for someone who has died; I am his vessel. Temba tells me something every day. He gives me guidance. He helped me find the man that killed him. The village punished him for his actions, he had to leave the village for a year to demonstrate his regret; this helped to heal the village. Temba helps me to help others every day. That is why I am called 'Temba.'" He stopped, wondering how Abigail would be able to hear his story. He sensed her father had been overwhelmed.

Abigail moved closer to him. She wanted to feel physically close to him like a neighboring tree touching the other's branches. She was silent for a time, feeling the full impact of what he had said. These were the conversations she had craved for over a year, this was the understanding she was looking for. As he spoke of Temba, Aunt Robin came into her mind, her beautiful wild-spirited Aunt whom she had loved like another parent and a best friend.

Finally she said, "That's beautiful, Temba. You're lucky to be carrying your uncle who you loved so much; and he's with you every day."

"He is with me every day, Abigail," he said, smiling, his heart filling with feelings for this young white girl. "If he wants my full attention, he comes like a butterfly in my ear and then I stop and focus fully. Every day he drops messages into my mind. I know they are his because I am not thinking about anything and then suddenly a thought is just sitting there. It feels like there is a hole in my head and Temba blows the message in."

Temba took Abigail's arm gently and pointed to the river now in view. "Do you see the place where there are rapids, all the white foam? It is the place where the river wakes up. We will sit under the jacaranda tree and then you can tell me your story." His grip was a little firmer now, but Abigail surrendered to his guidance. She felt love all around her, as if someone had helped her to find her way here. She felt dazed by his description of information dropping into his head. It was exactly how she experienced it. Could it possibly be her aunt, could it be Aunt Robin who was still with her after all this time? Her heart leaped at the thought. But what about the smoke over the dog? How could that be explained? She couldn't wait to get to the river and sit under the tree and tell her story. She couldn't leave today without knowing about the smoke and the voices. She wanted certainty that she was not going mad as her mother had thought, that she didn't have that S illness, that she wasn't a bad person for having these experiences. She needed answers, and Zukah (who was now Temba) would be the one to tell her. It scared her how much she needed from Temba. What if he didn't know? Quickly she pushed that thought out of her mind; with all this love around her she would trust that he had the answers; and the biggest dung beetle ball, that hadn't gone away like the others, would finally disappear.

Josef pointed out his hut to Bill. "We will go inside; the sun is at its fiercest now."

Bill followed; he felt young, very young next to this man. He had always passed the time of day with Josef but had never had a full conversation. Their children were the reason they had connected. He was pleased that both he and Josef had understood that Abigail and Zukah had an unusual bond and had both protected it. He considered Josef a traditional African. Bill felt a strong camaraderie with the African friends he had made at work, but they discussed politics and their work lives. He realized now he had only superficially dived into the culture; none of them appeared "traditional" to him. Perhaps they were and he'd chosen not to explore or see the differences. The arena they operated in was a white arena; it was his world, a white world, full of people in commercially dictated roles discussing the latest news. Everyone knew what was expected of him or her; it made the cross-cultural divide easy for him. Now he felt off-balance. He felt he was the equivalent of a son to Josef, even though they were similar ages. The feeling perplexed him; he hadn't had it before. He didn't even know what they would talk about after they had discussed their children.

The hut was bigger than he had imagined and very cool. There was bedding on the one side of the hut, and white enamel dishes collected on the other side. He noticed the hollow in the middle where a fire was built for cooking. The floor was spotless, not a leaf or a speck of collected dirt in sight. Josef pointed out two wooden stools in the center around the hollow and encouraged Bill to sit down. He went over and took two enamel mugs and a pot, which must have hot tea in it, Bill imagined. Bill was curious about the timing: how had Josef known he had just arrived? But the coincidence quickly left his mind. He felt awkward, as if his body were too big for the stool, as if he were out of his depth with this ancient man hovering around him.

Josef coughed. "Boss Boyd ...."

Bill interrupted nervously, "Please call me Bill, Josef; thank you for the tea," he clenched the cup firmly.

"Bill, what is it that troubles your daughter? She is a good person, a wise girl."

"Aah, Josef, it has been a difficult time. We don't understand her. We want to understand her, but she talks of things we know nothing about. We don't know how to guide her; she wants our guidance, but we're confused sometimes what to say. Do you know what I mean?" Bill had spilled the words, relieved that a conversation had started.

Josef shook his head and hesitated. While Bill looked closely at his face, his brown eyes narrowed and a furrow formed on his forehead. He cocked his head to one side like a dog before it pounces on the ball. "She is your guide, Bill. Sometimes children can be bigger spirits than their parents. She takes you down a path to open you up, and so your understanding of the world is different. That is the way I see it," he said gently nodding his head in understanding.

Bill didn't know how to respond at first. This conversation was unlike any he'd had before. Josef spoke with such certainty and conviction that despite his gentle tone, Bill felt confronted. "No one has ever said that before," he responded, needing to buy time.

"We Africans, we see the world differently from you. We are spiritual people; we understand the spirit world. We believe many things that white culture would find strange," he ventured, shuffling on the stool to get more comfortable.

"I don't know what you mean, Josef. I have many African friends. We talk about Shona culture."

"You are an open man, a good man, Bill, and I see that. I don't know what you talk about to your African friends, but if you heard more about the spirit world, maybe you would understand Abigail, your daughter."

"Tell me some things about the spirit world, Josef, how you see things differently from me; I'm curious." Bill stretched out his legs and put his feet more firmly on the ground in preparation for whatever revelations might come.

"Aah, Mr. Bill, it is like this: You believe that when your relatives die they go to heaven or hell. You put them in the ground and they are no longer with you, they have gone to heaven or hell and left you; you will not see them again until you die. This is a very strange idea for Shona people. We believe our dead are all around; they are with us every day. They are helping us, sharing their wisdom if we make the time to listen. Our ancestors would be angry with us if we ignored them like your culture does. Many of us are mediums, vessels for our ancestors, and we honor their wisdom. They guide us."

Bill shuffled in his seat, and pressed his feet more firmly on the ground to stabilize himself. "I don't understand how you would have contact, how a dead person can talk. How does this relate to my daughter?" He felt his chest tighten.

"Your daughter is a shaman: she hears and sees spirits. I have known that for a long time. Her ancestors who have died talk to her by dropping words in her head. She knows that they are not her thoughts. She is a wise one, but she is scared; she is an African shaman living in white culture. This is difficult for her."

Bill sputtered, "A shaman." He tried to say it calmly but it came out like a piece of dirt in his mouth that he was spitting out.

"Yes, a shaman," Josef repeated, holding firm.

"What does this mean for my daughter?" Bill asked quickly, desperate to be reassured that she would be all right and that this was not an illness.

"It means Abigail has the ability to lead. She has a gift. Honor her gifts; she has a lot to share. She is a strong spirit."

"Will she be OK? This isn't like an illness?" Bill felt ashamed asking, but he needed the reassurance that his daughter wasn't going mad, that she wouldn't take pills again, that his darling girl would be safe.

"No, Mr. Bill. I am explaining this is a gift. She has many talents. She is already guiding your family, opening you up to a different world, the spirit world. I know you are a Christian and you go to church, I am curious how your faith gives you strength?"

"We believe God gives us strength, if we ask. Maybe it's Him who kept our family going through all this. Maybe if I'd prayed more, if I'd told her to pray ..." Bill shook the regret from his head like a dog shaking water from its fur. "But as long as Abigail will be OK. You're telling me that with these abilities she will be OK, is that right Josef?" Bill rocked back and forth, trying to integrate all he had heard. He felt shattered, overwhelmed, as if a waterfall were crashing over his head and the bubbles were immersing his mind in liquid.

"Yes, your daughter will be fine, but will *you* be OK, Mr. Bill?" Josef asked compassionately, raising his mug to his mouth.

"Josef, I'm scared, scared that my daughter has abilities that will be hard for her." Bill's voice picked up speed as he spoke.

"It is harder for you, Bill, for your wife and other children. Abigail is used to her ability now, but she needs support. This is what my guides tell me: she needs you to accept her for who she is, not question why she knows what she knows. Accept her and her abilities."

"I will try, Josef." Bill didn't know what else to say. This was all too much. His daughter, a shaman? He wanted to show some openness, but he would need to think long and hard about what Josef was saying. It sounded as if his daughter, his baby, the family philosopher was a witchdoctor, and that scared the hell out of him.

"Mr. Bill, I would like to help you, and Temba, my son, he cares for your daughter; he can help her too, if she needs it. We can meet again."

"Aah, you are so kind, Josef, but we're leaving the country; it will be another year before we can come again." Bill bowed his head in deference.

Josef cupped his hands together. "Aah, I am sad you are leaving, but we will meet again. We are brothers, after all, in this strange country. We are brothers. Let us go to our children at the river and see what wild things have happened."

Bill stood up swaying, not understanding about wild things but following, following this man beside whom he felt shriveled, overwhelmed and destabilized, but grateful. He felt off-center, each footstep tentatively following the next on uncertain terrain in a changed world.

Chapter 17

The jacaranda tree hovered like a whimsical spirit, dancing in the wind above the two human forms. As its branches swayed, its shadows danced below, rushing over four legs spread out on the ground, touching the tops of two heads with a flirting sweep. The pair of young people were unaware of the dance above them, so locked were they in conversation with each other. Their eyes fixated on one another; the world around them had disappeared, even the river gushing excitedly in front, mimicking a sound of joy as its bubbles burst over the rocks.

"When did you start hearing voices, Abigail? Was it after the smoke?" Temba inquired, giving all of his attention to the moment.

"It was after the smoke. Are you sure that the smoke and the voices are Aunt Robin, Temba, are you sure?" she pleaded, wanting so much to believe it.

"Yes, you are a vessel for Robin, just as I am for Temba. I do not see Temba, I only hear him, but you have both seeing and hearing gifts. You are very lucky, Abigail; the spirits have blessed you with many abilities."

Abigail's tears eased out slowly at first from the corners of her green eyes; and then those tears seemed to make way for the others that had been stored inside for so long. As she cried, she felt wave upon wave of relief; finally she had been understood! As the tears rolled out, she felt the loneliness and confusion easing. She felt heaviness coming off her heart; her mind was clearer, space was forming, as if a big dung beetle ball had finally dissolved. Aunt Robin had been with her all this time.

Temba put his hand on her shoulder. He wanted her to lean into his body, but he didn't know what a black boy and a white girl should be doing. He wanted to be her baobab, a tree with such large branches that he could shelter her from some aspects of her culture, from all the judgment she had endured in telling her story to ears that repelled her experience. He wanted to hover over her; protect her from the winds of misunderstanding and rejection.

"Look, Abigail," he said to her. "Look at the river."

Abigail looked up and saw fish leaping out where the foam was gathering. Just then two cape doves swooped into the river and dipped their heads in the foam, their feathery bodies intermingling as if putting on a nature show. Everything was alive, bubbling and bursting. She suddenly looked behind her and in the distance saw two shadowy figures walking side by side on the dusty path. She looked closer at the male forms coming down the path and saw that two worlds were colliding, a white world and a black world; they were merging, forming and reforming. The world they made was fluid and uncertain of its shape, but it was expanding, expanding the idea of what was possible when the desire for human understanding was stronger than any other force, when a black man's and a white man's hearts and minds were open, open to discover each other's worlds with a curiosity so fierce it could light the sky.

CPSIA information can be obtained at www.ICGtesting.com
Printed in the USA
BVOW07s2156120914

366480BV00001B/2/P

9 780761 864264